ROYAL
BEAUTY
BRIGHT

a novel of World War I

ROYAL BEAUTY BRIGHT

a novel of World War I

RYAN BYRNES

Blank Slate Press | St. Louis, MO

Blank Slate Press
Copyright © 2019 Ryan Byrnes
All rights reserved.

For information, contact info@amphoraepublishing.com

Manufactured in the United States of America
Publication date: November 5, 2019
Cover Design by Kristina Blank Makansi

Cover Art: Shutterstock
ISBN: 9781943075607

For the Precious of the Earth

CHRISTMAS EVE, 1914
THE WESTERN FRONT

~ RODNEY STOKER ~

"I need a volunteer to lead the patrol tonight." Captain Blanding marched toward us, boots caked up to the ankle in mud. We'd been making the most of tea time—spooning a bit of stew out of our helmets. We'd learned to eat slow and waste nothing, relishing every morsel and lingering over very drop. He stopped next to our huddled group.

"Appleby, can I trust you with an officer's patrol?"

Why the captain even asked was a question for the ages. Every bloke knew that when an officer "asked" for volunteers, the answer was always the same.

"Yessir." Appleby swallowed hard. He'd worn a target on his back ever since that one night he got plastered and wandered into the captain's quarters.

"Pick your squad. Be out soon as it's dark," Blanding ordered. Before he turned to leave, his gaze fell on me. "Stoker, you'll take second in command." He gave me a curt nod. "Be careful, men."

Everyone rushed to finish eating, wiped their helmets clean, packed their things, and hurried back to business before Appleby could decide on his squad.

"Looks like I'm going with you, mate." I shrugged. "I figure we've had luck together so far, right?"

"You're a real pal, Rodney," Appleby clapped a palm on my shoulder.

"I'll go, too." Luther looked up from where he was huddled in a dark corner, arms wrapped around his rifle.

Luther? Volunteering?

"Certainly not," I said. "Luther, you're to stay in the trench."

Appleby frowned. "We'll see who else we can get, but if we're short volunteers, we'll have to take him."

"He'll only get in the way," I protested.

"No!" Luther shook his head. "If you're going, Rodney Stoker, I'm going, too."

Good lord, I just hoped he wasn't going to start rocking and flapping. He didn't do it often anymore, but when he did, it was hard to calm him down.

Appleby sighed. "Rodney, we may not have a choice."

Turned out, there were no volunteers. Fancy that. So we impressed Wallace, Wright, Somers, and Nash because they were the only ones who hadn't yet cleared the dugout. With Luther, we had a patrol. As each person went off to try and prepare for, or rather, distract themselves from, what might pass come nightfall, I caught up with Luther, who was now heading back to his post.

"You didn't have to do that," I said.

No response. As usual.

"Hey, listen to me." I grabbed his shoulder and pulled him around to face me.

He reared back, nostrils flaring. For some reason, I got the idea he was going to hit me, so I snapped my hand back and took a step away. Luther looked down on me.

"You're still afraid of me, Rodney Stoker."

"Th—that's beside the point. Listen, you need to get someone else to go on the patrol tonight, okay? You don't know what you're getting yourself into."

"I do know." He took a step toward me. "You think I'm daft, that I don't know because I'm different than you. But I do know. I know a lot."

"Bollocks. If you know so much, why'd you go and volunteer?"

No answer.

"Luther, have you any idea how bloody lucky you are? How many people are rooting for you to survive all this?" I gestured at the filthy trench we were stuck in. I hadn't planned on giving a monologue or anything of the sort, but the words just spilled out. "Since you arrived in November, things have been pretty quiet. If you play your cards right, you can make it to Christmas without actually seeing any combat, and then maybe Ethyl's letters to High Command will earn you a free ticket home. But a guy like me? I'm stuck here for three more years—three. If I get hurt, they'll just patch me up and keep sending me out to the front until I don't come back. And if I'm still breathing, but too injured to keep fighting, they'll amputate a leg or an arm or give me a new face and send me home to live with a bunch of civilians who'll look at me with pity and tell me to buck up and have a stiff upper lip when I can't find a job or when I close my eyes only to see all the men I've shot parading in front of me."

I was surprised those words came out of me—it sounded treasonous, mutinous, like old Tommy Wright from back home. What would my father say? He wouldn't countenance cowardice.

Luther sniffled and hung his head. "I just want to help so you won't have to be afraid anymore."

"'Don't you worry about me, Luther. Look after yourself. That's your job."

"But I do worry, Rodney Stoker. I worry about everything. All the time."

My words had bounced off him. I was a little bird tweeting at an elephant. Soon, we arrived at his post—a gap in the sandbags through which he'd stick his rifle and pretend to aim out of. He'd managed to fashion a little bench into the dirt wall, now frozen solid, and a small shelf where he kept an assortment of round marbles rolled out of mud. He saw me look at them and simply said, "Truffles. For Mum."

Then he looked like he was going to cry, so I decided to change the subject. "Do you write to your mum?"

His eyes widened, and he shook his head. "I don't know my letters."

"Doesn't she write you?"

"I don't know my letters."

I swallowed. I remembered Mrs. Baker from the candy shop. She'd always given me the collywobbles. Damned if I knew why. According to Father Carmichael, she'd carried me in her arms all the way through the village when Luther gave me a nasty concussion. We were just young lads then, but in all the years since, I'd never thanked her. I was pretty sure Mrs. Baker hated my parents. And that the feeling was mutual.

"What about if I write for you, Luther?" I asked him. "What if I help you write your mum? Would you like that?"

He touched his throat, feeling the lump in it, and swallowed. He exhaled a few times, heavily, his breath a cloud in the cold.

"Alright, alright, no crying."

That comment didn't go over well, and Luther started in on the weird noises.

"Jesus, Mary, and Joseph! Cut the cackle, now will you?" I snapped my fingers close to his nose, and he crossed his forearms over his eyes, surprised.

"But what will you write, Rodney Stoker?"

"Whatever you tell me. In fact, let's do it right now. Hold on."

I trudged down the trench, through puddles in the thick chalk mud that still hadn't managed to freeze, over to where Mo Bipton, our own Royal Warwickshire poet, sat scribbling with his pencil and paper. After a short negotiation, starting with four cigarettes, we managed to make a trade—six cigarettes for stationery and a pencil. I rushed the supplies back over to Luther, who was eyeing his new creation, a mud truffle-pyramid, with a furrowed brow.

"Alright, so what do you want me to write?"

Luther ran a hand through his hair, and his fist stopped to tug on it, palm resting on his forehead.

"Tell her, um, tell her," he squirmed in his seat, popping his knees up and sitting on his heels, "tell her I, tell her that I, I—" He paused, clicking his tongue and staring off into the distance.

"Tell her what, Luther?" I rolled my eyes. "We can't be here all day; we have a patrol to prep for."

"I don't know! What do you want me to say?"

"Whatever you want, God almighty!" Blood rushed to my face, and I was surprised at myself. I was usually able to keep calm no matter what, but Luther took a lot of patience. And maybe the patrol worried me more than I wanted to admit.

"Let's just write it later," he said.

"No. We're writing it now."

"I don't know what she wants to hear. I've never written a letter. Let's talk about the patrol."

"Alright," I exhaled. "We can write your mum tomorrow. Here's what we're going to do on the patrol tonight. There will be seven of us, and Appleby is in charge."

"Appleby?"

"Yes, John Appleby. You know, the bloke you just volunteered to go out with."

"I know him."

I drew in a long breath. "Are you sure? He's tall, got a thick mustache. Straw-colored hair. Missing his pinky."

"Missing his pinky. I know."

I could never be sure what Luther knew or didn't know, but I went on. "Okay. So we're going to crawl across No Man's Land when it gets dark, crater to crater, until we get to the listening post. We'll stay there and listen for a few hours, then come back before sunrise. Here are the rules. Luther, hey."

He'd reached down and scraped up a handful of mud and started rolling more out more of his truffles. His eyes closed as he felt the little balls between his palms. I snapped my fingers in his face again, and he looked at me.

"Here are the rules. Stay behind me at all times, especially if you hear gunfire. If I'm not there, hide behind Appleby or one of the others. If you're alone, hide in a crater and stay there until the patrol finds you come daylight. Luther, listen to me. A dozen German rifles are trained on any given point along this trench. Draw attention to yourself in any way, and there go your chances of seeing your mum again."

"I know," he said. Then he closed his eyes and started rolling more mud balls and setting them gently on his truffle shelf. I watched for a moment, then got up and left.

About an hour after supper—maybe five, maybe six— the sky bruised to red, then purple, after which we had only the moonlight's glint off the frozen chalk mud to see by. We gathered where we knew the machine gunners would give us cover fire if needed. We stripped off our heavy overcoats and left them in a pile; everyone knows that heavy coats slow you down when you're trying to run. Plus if we didn't make it back from the patrol, there'd be free coats for the freezing blokes who needed them. In just my khaki uniform, I hugged myself, breathing into my hands for warmth. My fingers were purple and cracked and shaking; my breath clouded about me.

"Ready?" Appleby asked, passing his cigarette butt to one of the gunners.

"Yep," I nodded. It was a lie we all told ourselves.

"Right." Appleby took a breath and stepped up the first rung of the ladder.

He poked his head out of the trench. No gunfire. One second later, he rolled over the edge and flattened himself by a line of sandbags and a coil of barbed wire. Wallace stepped up to the ladder as well. One or two cold drops struck my neck, and I noticed flakes in the swirling filth at the bottom of the trench. Snow.

CHRISTMAS EVE, 1914

THE PORT OF LE HAVRE

~ THE PORT ~

The black waves of the English Channel erupted with spittle and foam. Warships chugged through the churning crests, every square foot of the decks crammed with khaki-clad soldiers. "Mind the ice," they'd mumble, pointing out slicks on the stairways and ten-foot icicle stalactites on the smokestacks. They congregated under tarps to pass cigarettes and play cards while the port of Le Havre slowly emerged from the fog. The medieval city walls hinted at a time of wooden ships and cannonballs, though recently reinforced with artillery nozzles peeking from concrete pillboxes.

For longer than even the oldest citizens could remember, Christmas tree ships would arrive in Le Havre from the forests of Norway, and salesmen dragged out bundles of spruces, standing them in rows under green banners that read: *Marché de l'Sapin de Noël*. Mothers towed babbling children to the makeshift Christmas tree market to *ooh* and *aah*, and in the evening, salesmen set out oil lamps around the trees so that the little forest twinkled.

"Maman, je veux que, je veux que," toddlers squealed, pointing chubby fingers at their chosen tree.

"Vous devez être bonne cette année," mothers replied, and because the good boys and girls knew Pére Noël was watching—Pére Noël in his red cloak and his bulging belly, tugging a bag of gifts—the children would try so very hard to be kind. On the way back home, they would offer to carry the tree even though it was thrice their height. They would offer to help their grandmothers cross the roads where the armored cars rattled and the soldiers marched. When babies cried at the distant sound of heavy artillery, they would press lips to the smooth cheeks in an attempt to quell tears.

Mothers and grandmothers pulled their children close as they passed the alleys where refugees crouched in the shadows. They had made the pilgrimage from as far as Belgium and had erected shanty-towns near street-corners, near brothels, near the steps of churches.

Some churches, boasting gothic arches and flying buttresses, glowed with colored light from within, adorned with banners of purple and pink, wreaths of green and red, and constellations of candles. There were the advent candles of peace, hope, joy, and love. There were candles in remembrance of family members long dead. And there were the candles lit by nuns whispering prayers for an end to the war.

From the single-room slum flats to the red-brick rowhouses, families strung their evergreens with ornaments of folded newspaper and straw; they had donated their metal ornaments for bullet-making.

Grandmothers left Yule logs by fireplaces, and children laid out their shoes at the hearth. Mothers sat their children down and told them stories from rocking chairs, while suckling their babes under their shawls. These women told the children that if they were good and kind, Pére Noël would leave special gifts in their shoes that would make them forget the whole war. But only if they followed the new rules. First, they must not talk to the soldiers or play outside during the day anymore. They could only go outside when Mama was there. Big boys could go outside when looking for scrap metal to sell, but only the big boys, not the little boys or little girls. If the rules were broken, the good boys and good girls would become bad and Pére Fouettard would slide down the chimney instead of Pére Noël, bringing his whip for the bad boys and bad girls. The children lay on their bellies while they listened, brows creased, heads propped up on their palms.

"Quand papa rentre à la maison?" the little boys would ask.

The mothers would reply it was not the time to ask when Papa would return. Right then was the time to tell stories. And so the mothers would tell their children stories of baby Jesus, of how farm animals spoke to each other on Christmas Eve, of kindly ghosts that return to the living, of how wars eventually end and people live together again. Outside, more ships docked. More soldiers and trucks and armored cars rolled by on their way to the front.

~ JIM BAKER ~

When we docked at Le Havre, I was in the cargo hold of a big steamer, crammed wall to wall with post sacks. I'd passed most of the Channel crossing talking to a gent named Gibson, a stout fellow assigned to guard the post. A son was born to him six months ago, he explained with great enthusiasm, showing me the photographs.

"My second child. Little man's probably crawling by now." He flashed me a grayscale snapshot of a wee potato of a baby dressed up in a bonnet.

"I don't suppose you've met him yet?"

He shook his head no. I think I learned everything there was to know about babies as I sat there next to Gibson, hugging my knees and praying the ship would stop rocking.

"You married?" Gibson asked. "Got any children of your own."

"I have an older brother, Luther, but sometimes I think he might as well be a child."

Gibson slapped me on the back and roared with laughter for what must have been the fifth time.

"What, is your brother a lawyer?"

"He makes candy."

Gibson threw his head back like it was the funniest thing he'd ever heard.

"Now he's a soldier. I'm actually on my way to see him."

"Duty calls, I suppose."

I could have spat just then. What did he know about anything? This soft bloke's only job in the world was to sit on a boat and make sure nobody stole the bloody post. Who would want to steal a letter, anyway? I wanted to tell him that Luther wasn't like other men, that he'd been tricked into joining up and was drafted illegally, and that I'd come to spring him from the army and put him on a boat to Algeria, but I kept silent. A drop of water landed on my neck, so all I said was, "Is this boat leaking?"

"Boy, there's less a chance of this boat catching a leak than a U-boat blowing us to Davy Jones' locker."

What?

We sat together in the cargo hold with the post sacks for another few hours, and eventually I tried closing my eyes but never could fall asleep. Whenever a wave bashed against the hull, the sacks shifted, and the dissolved fish and chips from my last meal sloshed around in my stomach.

"You nervous, son?" Gibson asked. "About fighting in France, I mean."

"No, no," I shook my head. "I mean, I won't see any fighting. I'll just be a postman. Behind the lines, you know. I'm taking a train to Hazebrouck to fill a position as a lorry driver. Completely safe."

This time, Gibson didn't laugh.

A while later, the engines quieted, and Gibson's head shot up. "That'll be the shallows. We'll be there soon."

When the whistle blew, I slung my bag over my shoulders, then checked the holstered pistol at my side. Still hadn't the faintest notion of how to use it, but somehow it made me feel official.

"Hey," Gibson called. "Good luck out there. Keep your wits. Take care of that brother of yours."

"Yeah, thanks," I nodded, starting up the ladder.

I'd always considered myself an introvert. I liked people well enough, I guess, except when I was surrounded by them. Seemed like there were a thousand soldiers up on deck, the whole lot of them talking at the same time. Reinforcements heading for the front was what I'd been told.

Whatever, they were infantrymen, and I was an engineer, so I avoided eye contact, pushed up my sleeves— even though it was cold and foggy—and puffed out my chest and pushed through the crowd to the edge of the ship where I saw the city of Le Havre for the first time. Some sailors lowered the gangplank, and I was among the first to file off.

They frowned at me and let off a string of nasal gibberish, then returned to their work lugging crates. *Oh yeah, French. Damn.* But I'd learned a little French in school, one or two phrases, at least, and now was a good chance to put them to use.

"Wait!" I called after them again. "The *bureau de poste*, where is it? *Bureau de poste.*"

They laughed and pointed down the dock. I stood there after they left, just looking around. Was I supposed to just go? I felt like there must be some rule preventing me from walking away from the soldiers and heading out on my own. But nobody seemed to be paying attention to me, so I headed out, lugging my bag through a maze of crates and containers and shipyard material.

The crowd of soldiers shrank behind me, and still nobody was coming after me, asking me what the hell I was doing, because I had no idea. The rain picked up, and I stopped to pull the oilcloth coat out of my bag and wrap it around my shoulders. I walked by more crates and more crates, and eventually found a cluster of warehouses at the end of the dockyard. I cupped my hands to peek through the windows and see if there was anything there. More crates.

It had been ten minutes, and I was already lost.

Should I head back to the ship and find someone who speaks English? I turned around and the ship was barely visible in the fog. So I kept searching, and after peeking around corners for another twenty minutes, I found an alley that led into a street full of marching soldiers, the same soldiers from the ship, I figured. And there, right in front of me, was a warehouse with a sign hanging above the doorway: BRITISH ARMY POSTAL SERVICE.

Now all that stood in my way was a short train-ride to the frontlines, where I would be assigned a posts lorry, get a map, drive to the front, and find Luther. I just hoped my information was good, and that he was still where the clerks told me he'd been assigned. Would he remember me? I hadn't seen him in about seventeen years. What was that, 1897? Blimey. That was almost half a lifetime ago.

DECEMBER, 1897
LEAMINGTON SPA, ENGLAND

~ THE VILLAGE ~

All along Bath Street, men in tweed caps and woolen sweaters nailed evergreen wreaths on shutters as housewives bundled in well-worn cardigans framed doorways with garlands and set candles in windowsills. Inside the snug row houses of Georgian red brick, sons and daughters unwrapped the newspaper protecting heirloom glass decorations and carefully arranged the family nativity scene on the mantle.

Only the storefront of Baker's Sweets was quiet. No tree, no tinsel, no candlelit nativity, no evergreen. The only activity was the hanging sign creaking in the blustering wind announcing "Boiled Sweets. Toffee. Handmade Fudge. Since 1821."

On bright warm days during the summer tourist season, Bath Street would swell with handholding newlyweds, old men in top hats, beggars, earls, fine ladies, artists, scientists, and cripples, all come to visit the mineral springs at the nearby Royal Baths. Many carried pamphlets proclaiming the baths could cure lameness, blindness, even diseases of the brain. The crowds appeared every year, hobbling on canes from shop to shop. *Hobble, hobble, stop. Hobble, hobble, stop.* They would circulate through Baker's Sweets and speak to Mrs. Constance Baker behind the counter, who nodded and smiled and pretended to care.

"So how did you come by the candy trade? It's a rare day for a woman to run such a business all by herself."

Mrs. Baker would paste on a smile. "I inherited the store when my husband died."

"Goodness. Well." Awkward silence usually followed, and then. "Do you ever take the baths? Are they as helpful as everyone says?"

"I tried them for my son. He has fits."

"Oh, I'm terribly sorry to hear that. Did they help?"

"How many pieces of marzipan did you want?"

The sick and lame and their caretakers would come every day for a week, growing more and more sullen each day, and when their holiday ended, Constance would wave them on, saying, "Now, remember to come back next year. You'll be healed for sure. Why, I can see you stepping lighter already." And when the newlyweds strolled in, or handsome, broad shouldered bachelors walked through looking for a gift for a particular sweetheart, Miss Baker would try out her cheeriest voice. "Oh, buy some bonbons, why won't you? Just made 'em this morning." And they would buy. All the tourists bought from Baker's Sweets. Everybody who did not know her bought from her.

Yet when the leaves blushed every autumn and the tourists had all taken their leave, the store fell quiet. Constance ran her business mostly through the mail, packaging and mailing sweets all around the countryside. She wouldn't see many locals again until Christmastime, and even then it would just be a few housewives without the time or the talent to do their own baking. Sometimes, if they couldn't find a babysitter, they'd drag their children along and peruse the aisles of pink bonbons, marzipan, mints, saltwater taffy, and the ever-enduring British toffee. Then they would reach over the counter, avoiding an accidental brush of the fingers, snatch their paper bag, hold it away from their bodies like it was a dead rat, and slip off into the night. The doorbells would jingle behind them.

Sometimes, especially during the quiet of a winter's evening, neighbors would claim to hear shattering glass ring from the shop and echo down the street. On those nights, the neighbors would check the locks on their front doors and pull the blinds shut.

~ CONSTANCE BAKER ~

The bells jingled over the door, and I looked up from the fudge I was cutting to see, of all people, Margie Stoker and her son step inside. *Why, God? What does she want from me now?* How is it she had to come at this hour, ten minutes before closing? Especially—my chest tightened—when I'd just let Luther down to play in the kitchen. Oh, well, it was too late to do anything about that now.

I squeezed the knife and put on that familiar smile that made my cheeks sore. Margie nodded and smiled back, unwinding her scarf as she stamped the sludge off of her shoes, onto my floor, and crossed the welcome mat. I'd kick her out—or at the least, fantasize about it—if it wasn't for the jingling music in her purse. She took a few steps and frowned, looking at the bottom of her shoe like she'd stepped in dog poo. I knew what she was looking at. It had been an unusually busy day, and the floor was littered with crumbs dropped by posh neighbors, reluctant customers who turned up their noses at me and expected me to grab a broom every time they deigned to enter the premises. *Sorry, I haven't had the time to clean yet today, everyone. I've been busy.*

Her eyes took in the tray of fudge beneath my knife. I swallowed, preparing to say something in case she started a conversation. My heart thumped in my chest, and I realized that, in some deep part of me, I was still a little girl afraid of a typical class bully.

The floorboards creaked as Margie and her boy stepped behind a shelf. The beam holding up the low ceiling shivered as a gust of wind whipped down the street. Behind the shelf, she cleared her throat and whispered just for effect. It was a small store, after all. Too small for secrets.

"How about the licorice, Rodney? You think Daddy would like that?"

"He wouldn't like that very much, mummy. Nobody likes licorice."

"Your Daddy likes licorice very much, actually. It's his favorite."

"But licorice for Christmas?"

"Hey, fingers out of your mouth. It's not clean."

Rodney made a few garbled sounds.

A slap and a whimper.

"Sorry."

"Here, I'll just grab some of these. Go look over at the bonbons while I buy this, and don't touch anything. It's not clean."

A rush of feet on the creaking wood signaled little Rodney skipping to the back. *Oh no you don't.* I stood on my toes to see the kid skip over to the back corner, next to the taffy hook near the kitchen door. *If you even think about going in there...* I squeezed the handle of my fudge knife even harder, tracing a line through the chocolate and pinching the squares with wax paper.

"It's dim in here, don't you think?" Margie stepped up to the counter, set down a half pound of licorice, and handed me the coins. "Rather dreary for a sweet shop."

"Indeed."

Rodney's little head kept poking over the bonbon shelves.

I closed a hand over the change.

"It's a shame this is the only sweet shop in town."

I smiled. "Have a good evening, Mrs. Stoker."

Margie grabbed her bag of licorice, and winding her scarf back around her neck, she headed for the door.

"Rodney, dear, time to go. Rodney?"

His head had disappeared from behind the shelf. And then, Rodney's trembling voice called from the kitchen.

"Wh—who're you?"

A deep moan, and the clatter and crash of something thrown against the wall.

Christ Almighty. My knife dropped. I slipped out from behind the counter, pushed past the gaping Margie and the curious Rodney, and stepped into the kitchen. There was my son, nine years old and in his underwear, standing on the table with a pot in each hand. He tottered forward and, with a pale flabby arm, waved one at Rodney. Petrified, Rodney backed into the corner.

"Pity's sake, he's not the devil, Rodney. What're you shrinking away for?"

Luther swayed back and forth, waving the pots, shouting gibberish.

"He sounds like a sick cow!"

I whirled on Margie as her hand flew up to cover her mouth. I could feel the heat in my face and would have socked her about then. I would have, I swear. Luther saw straight past me, now that Margie entered the kitchen. Sometimes I felt like we were all just targets for him to chuck pots at.

I walked up and grabbed the pots, but he held them tight and started jerking his head forward and back so hard it had to hurt his poor neck. Once he started doing that, I knew from experience there was nothing I could say or do to calm him. I didn't even know if he could hear me. I grabbed him by the waist and heaved him off the table, back toward the tea-room as he flailed his arms and chucked a pot at Rodney. I hoped it hit the brat. Luther kept a tight grip on the other pot, the one he was trying to hit his head with, and as I tried again to snatch it away, he let out a shriek, banged his head against my already bruised shoulder, and kicked me in the thigh. I bent over, wincing, and exhaled all my anger. *Love him sweet*, I recited my motto, *love him sweet*. These episodes used to leave me in an impassioned mess, but that kind of energy had fizzled out of me years ago. Handling him now was purely mechanical, and when his shouts rose, I'd sigh and march over to him, a bit more hollowed out each time.

Dragging the last pot out of his grasp and sending it crashing in the corner, I laid Luther on the rug and threw down the pillows from the couch. He jumped to his feet, made fists, and screamed so loud his body spasmed and red veins stuck out of the taught-rope muscles on his neck. Then he started punching himself in the head.

In the doorway to the tea room—*they had followed us for a spectacle*—Margie pulled Rodney close and covered his ears.

I grappled with Luther to hold his arms down, but he pulled away, grabbed his temples, and rocked back and forth like there was a demon inside. *Was he in pain? Would I ever know what was going on in his mind?*

Finally, I pinned him down on the pillows and laid my body parallel to his, staring straight at him. His eyes, still wild, saw straight past me. He continued to rage and spasm, even kicking me a few times. With eyes closed, I lay there for about five minutes, pretending I was a statue. His hoarse voice simmered down to his regular blubbering gibberish, and I felt him calm down to that steady *thump thump thump* as his heart rate slowed and, finally, Luther made his little baby whimper, his happy sound, to signal the episode's passing. I got up, as I did about three times a week, looked him in the eye, and watched as the spark of recognition returned. He was listening.

"Are you sorry?" I asked.

He whined apologetically.

"Give me a kiss, love."

He pressed his mouth against my cheek, and I hugged him for a good thirty seconds until finally he hugged me back. I smelled the sweat on his skin and felt familiar tears on my cheek. I whispered a quick prayer to Luther's father in heaven.

Love him sweet, I told myself, *love him sweet*.

When I turned around, Margie and her son were gone. I'd be hearing from her come Sunday. The vicar would probably stop by with that concerned bend in his brow, and I'd have to explain again why no, he couldn't stay for tea and discuss my son's behavior. And so the gossip would pour forth for the enigma of Leamington Spa, sometimes a subject of sympathy, and other times judgement. Yes, it was true that my son acted out. Yes, it was true that I wasn't interested in re-marrying. What's it matter to them what goes on under my roof?

I dropped into the chair and rubbed my temples. Luther stood and began to run circles around the house, making sounds to himself until he tired. I smiled as he opened the cupboard door near the oven—the only cupboard I hadn't fastened under lock and key—and curled up inside it, shutting himself in. He napped in there. I guess small spaces made him feel safe, maybe like the womb. My eyes closed for a few minutes, and the *bong bong bong* of the grandfather clock startled me awake. Heavens, I hadn't yet locked up shop. Two steps in the shop, and the bell rattled, the door opened, and there stood Jim. He stepped in with no pants, no shoes, feet covered in snow.

"What is this? What *is* this?"

I grabbed his chin and squeezed it like I'd done the fudge knife earlier. Pointed his face left and right and then straight at me, and there was his eye all swollen and purple.

"You've been out picking fights again, haven't you? Must be the third time they've taken your pants."

"They were making fun of Luther, Mum. Making fun of how he is."

"Think losing your pants and shoes will make them stop?"

"No, I—"

I slapped him. I know I shouldn't have but, good lord, how much more of this was I supposed to take?

"Boys who pick fights are not gentlemen. You're the one person in this family with a future, and you're going to toss it all away! At only seven years old? How many pairs of pants do you have to lose before you learn? How many shoes? Hmm? Where do you think you'll be when you're my age? 'Cause I won't give you the shop if you're like this. The neighbors know it. Your Auntie Lavinia knows it."

"No she *doesn't.*"

Jim's voice cracked. I'd hit a soft spot when I mentioned Lavinia. It was probably too far. Jim reached out, and with one arm, he cleared the whole tray of fudge I'd been working on off the counter and onto the floor.

"Why, you—" I raised my hand again when I heard that terrible, hoarse whimpering that made me cringe. I turned around, and there was Luther behind me, shaking and smacking his head over and over again.

Time to get the pillows back out.

Jim raced up the stairs and locked himself in his room, where I knew I'd find him curled up, hiding under his covers with one of his father's books. That's what he did whenever I lost my temper or Luther had one of his episodes. He never offered to help. He just hid.

Below the red brick clock tower with its white cap, the naked trees rattled. I dragged Luther along the gravel path.

"Stop that blubbering. If you want to talk, use words."

He made a baby whimper that sounded like "yah" and suddenly stopped, squatting down on his hams to poke a dead worm in the slush. He picked it up and started to put it in his mouth.

"*No.*"

The worm fell into the snow.

I pulled at Luther's hand, and he stood and hopped along with me, making that rubbery squeaking sound with his voice.

"Words." I stopped and enunciated. "No sounds. Words." He didn't make eye contact, but instead hugged himself and rocked on his heels, so I paused and pulled his face close to mine. "We're going to see a very important person today, and you need to behave."

He made an apologetic whimpering sound and hit himself, so I pulled his tubby body in close and hugged him until he calmed. The words *love mum* came through the garbling, and it may have been the most thrilling moment of my entire week. He put his mouth on my cheek. It sometimes felt strange, that a boy the same height as his mum still must hold hands. But I don't give a damn. *Love him sweet.*

We walked past a wood-post sign with carved letters painted in gold that read:

HATTON NORTHERN HOSPITAL
FOR LUNATICS AND THE FEEBLE-MINDED

Sometimes, when it was just me and Luther, which was a lot, I imagined having conversations with him. What would he be like if he was fully vocal? *Where are we going, Mum?* he might ask. *The Doctor's going to check up on you, love, it won't hurt*, I'd respond. But today his face was blank. He didn't know where he was, and he didn't ask.

"I love you, dear," I said and tussled the light brown hair I'd combed and washed that morning, six o'clock sharp, with him naked in the bath. I could tell his body was changing, and soon he would be a man with a man's arms and a man's chest and back and hands. Soon he would be of age, and I'd be unable to handle him. Truth be told, I had no idea how we'd get on then. Or later, when I was gone. Jim would have to look after him. He must, but I didn't actually think he would. Sometimes I think Luther's got more sense in his fits than Jim with all his faculties.

"I love you, dear," I repeated. He squatted down, not even hearing me. I pulled him to his feet and led him up the stone steps, between the red bricks and engraved grey cornerstones. After knocking on the large wooden door, so shined up I could see myself in it, a smiling man in a white suit answered it. He was maybe six feet tall, like a mountain with sloping shoulders and tree trunks stuck up his sleeves. There were red cuts on his knuckles. He looked down at us.

"Mrs. Baker?" His voice rumbled out like distant thunder. He looked around me as if he'd lost something. "Is your husband with you?"

"I am a widow." I corrected him.

"And you never remarried?"

"Not a chance."

He gave me a condescending frown as if living on my own was a serious character flaw.

"Very well. Dr. Newby has been awaiting you. Come this way."

The entrance hall was rather bright, despite my expectations. Potted plants, white tiled floor, and an electrical chandelier. Nice place to live. Luther's grip on my hand tightened, and he squirmed and rocked under the glare of the towering man.

"May I ask your name, sir?"

"Dibbs, ma'am."

"And what do you do here, Mr. Dibbs?"

"Whatever needs doing. Sometimes custodial work, sometimes I assist the administrators." He cleared his throat. "Sometimes I handle the patients."

I pursed my lips.

A flight of stairs later, we were at Dr. Newby's office.

"Welcome, welcome!"

Dr. Newby, decked out in a starched white coat and a smart bow tie, stepped from behind his desk. He shook my hand, then extended his hand to Luther, who just stared at it.

"Odd."

"He doesn't shake, Dr. Newby." I gripped my purse. Surely, a doctor should not be surprised by that. No matter. Dr. Newby invited us in. I took a seat in one of the leather chairs across from his desk, setting Luther in the other chair. He tried sitting in my lap, but it was awkward, considering he weighed more than me now.

"You're too big to sit in my lap, Luther."

He made that squeaking sound and squirmed into the fetal position on the other chair.

"Use your words," I whispered.

Behind us, Dr. Newby clicked the door shut.

"How were your travels? Not too much effort, I hope? Did you exert yourself?"

I laughed, much to Newby's disappointment. His eyes narrowed as he leaned against the corner of his desk, picking up a stack of papers with one hand and pulling at his mustache with the other.

"I received your second letter and did sufficient research before your arrival. Luther's case, I must say, intrigues me."

"So, do you have a diagnosis?"

"Yes, I'm afraid so."

Oh, God. "Let's hear it." My voice cracked at the end, and I swallowed hard.

"There are many grades of mental defectivities discussed in the halls of medicine, Mrs. Baker. Many require symptoms present at birth or manifesting at an early age. You have described behaviors in Luther that presented early and that I have classified as stunted moral, social, and intellectual development. For instance, you report that he has limited ability to return sentiment and an inability to perform basic tasks like tying shoes or attending to personal hygiene. If he is to function at his best, he needs constant attendance and vigilance at all hours of the day. By all accounts, Mrs. Baker, I am sad to inform you that your son fits the diagnosis for an imbecile and should be institutionalized before it's too late."

"What the bloody hell is that supposed to mean? Too late for what?"

Luther scratched at the stitching on the chair, and I quickly closed my hand over his.

Dr. Newby exhaled, took off his spectacles, and stowed them in his chest pocket.

"Mrs. Baker, I'm afraid you and your husband—"

"In my correspondence, I informed you that I am a widow."

"Oh, yes. Well, hmm." He cast a skeptical eye my way, probably wondering if I could make a decision without a husband to guide me. He cleared his throat. "Mrs. Baker, I really do feel your pain. I have given this talk to many parents, some sitting in the very seat you are in now. It comes as a shock, I know, and your mind is flooded with questions. What future does the child have? Are there cures? How did the disease originate? I will endeavor to educate you on this matter, but only partially, for I do not wish to further confuse an agitated mother such as yourself with complicated physiological treatises."

I gritted my teeth, said nothing, and nodded for him to continue.

"The works of the late Charles Darwin are under wide scrutiny these days, and this line of thinking has brought on many advances in science, such as the newfound theory known as eugenics. There are those who say that mental deficiency is a result of bodily mutation. Mutations occur all the time in nature, and some turn out to be advantageous, such as the growth of wings in birds, the ability for fish to breathe underwater. Sometimes, as is the case here, mutations occur in the mind that are of no advantage. In fact, they are a disadvantage. And in many of the cases in which a mutation of the mind has occurred, there is little hope of improvement."

Dr. Newby motioned toward Luther, still curled in a ball in the chair.

"And when there is little hope for improvement, Mrs. Baker, a parent's choices are limited. As your son gets older, you may be unable to handle him. You may, even, be threatened by him, by his very … physicality."

A fly buzzed through the cracked-open windowpanes behind the desk, and Luther watched it closely. I said nothing. Dr. Newby drew in a breath and continued.

"There are a wide variety of people on this planet, some more well adapted than others. Thankfully, the European, and the Englishman in particular, is the most well adapted, as evidenced by our history. We have had great men like Shakespeare, Newton, and even Mr. Darwin himself come from our stock. To ensure this continued evolution, we must make certain future generations are also of the best stock. For this reason, institutions such as this one are seen as places in which we must segregate out from the population those who should not, shall we say, be allowed in general society and who cannot be allowed to procreate and defile future generations. Therefore, such institutions practice strict sexual segregation, in the hopes that people such as your son will not bear offspring with his same deficiency."

"But he's still just a boy."

"Not for long, Mrs. Baker. It is highly recommended that Luther be placed here, within a professional, nurturing environment so he can be sterilized before he is of age."

Sterilized. I took a deep breath. "And just what will you do to him here?"

"Excuse me?"

"I mean to say, how will he be treated?"

Dr. Newby reached into the pocket of his white coat and pulled out a pack of cigarettes. He offered one to me, and I took it.

"There are many treatments available to Luther. I have found that fresh air is the best. A nice walk in the open air can calm most agitations. But when he has fits, like the ones you described, we use drug therapy, electroconvulsive therapy, hydrotherapy, and the ice cure."

"The ice cure?"

"Our nurses here will prepare a bath filled with ice and confine him to it for a few hours. Cold temperatures soothe the muscles and most major agitations, you see. The ice will clear his mind."

"What if that doesn't work?"

"It usually does. Mrs. Baker, I assure you, Luther will be in safe hands here."

"I never said he was coming here. I am only inquiring as to what his diagnosis is and what his treatment might be *if* he came here."

"Keeping him at home will only serve to prolong his fits, I'm afraid. It must be very taxing for you and your ... for you to carry on this way, Mrs. Baker."

"I carry on just fine, Doctor."

"But—"

"No buts. I will take what you've said under advisement."

"Mrs. Baker, I strongly suggest—"

"I understand what you suggest, Dr. Newby. To use your own words, I am not an imbecile."

I stood and Luther unfolded himself and got to his feet. With a curt nod and nothing more to say, I took Luther's hand and we left.

CHRISTMAS EVE, 1914
THE WESTERN FRONT

~ RODNEY STOKER ~

We didn't speak one word throughout the patrol—
we knew the Germans would be listening for us.
I followed Appleby's lead across No Man's Land, just like
they'd taught us in training. He held up an open palm
to signal for us to stop, and the other six of us crouched
slowly, thighs burning until we'd reached a squat. From
there, we lowered onto our bellies and crawled, taking care
to stick to the craters, where we could be sure the mines
had already detonated.

I held my rifle in front of me as we approached each
crater, peeking over the edge first to make sure no Germans were trapped inside. We found one German half
dead, and I distracted Luther while Wallace quietly did
the work nobody else wanted to, taking care to stuff a
cloth down his mouth first. Poor bloke. Once inside the
next crater, we waited until all seven of us had regrouped,
and we nodded at Appleby to poke his head over the edge
to decide what crater we would crawl to next. I caught
Luther's eye and pressed a finger to my lips. He'd left his

rifle slung over his back while we were crawling, and we could all hear it rattling as he crawled. I grabbed the gun and put it in his hands, signaling that he needed to keep it out, for his own safety. He trembled and smelled like piss. We all did. Appleby nodded and pointed over the edge, to where a tree trunk had fallen over some barbed wire, flattening it into a break we could crawl over. Beyond that was the shadow of another pit we would hide in. It looked like a good place to set up a listening post, to lay low while we waited for the German officers to give orders for the movements of troops and the timing of the next barrage.

Soon, it was time to go over. Appleby went first, then Wallace, Wright, Somers, and Nash. Before going over, I stepped to Luther and bent his arms so that he was holding the rifle properly and wouldn't get a cartridge in his eye. I tapped his forehead to remind him what I'd said earlier: *hear a gunshot, hide behind me.* I put a hand on his neck, and we stood there quiet for a few seconds. Then I left.

Between craters, I dragged myself across the wet ground, imagining I could hear the Earth's comforting heartbeat and that I was clinging to her, prostrating myself before her in the hope that she'd spare me. It reminded me what serenity was, being so close and so vulnerable to something so large and unshakeable. I knew then why the ancients prayed to an Earth Mother and not an Earth Father.

Up ahead, I watched Appleby's silhouette approach the fallen tree, where he stopped. My heart sped up. What if there was a mine under the tree? The tree was the only un-exploded object within a hundred meters. Appleby shook his head and crawled away, I guess suddenly realizing this.

Instead, he crawled down the line and chose an empty stretch of barbed wire, where he pulled out his wire cutters and started snipping away.

"*Oye!*" German voices.

Appleby's cutters fell from his fingers, and he covered his head in his hands. Everyone followed suit, except me. I glanced back at Luther, who was inching behind me just like I'd told him, except he sounded like a gamboling bear, and I could hear him sloshing through the mud. I signaled for him to make like a mouse, but he just kept crawling faster. I motioned for him to stop again and mouthed *Stop! They can hear you!*

Meanwhile, the Germans carried on their prattle, just fifty meters away in their trench. The prattle was good, I convinced myself. As long as the Germans were talking to each other, they wouldn't be listening for us. But just because some of them were talking didn't mean they all were. They had snipers, too. What were the snipers doing? Who were they watching?

Luther kept crawling, louder and louder. *Slosh, slosh, slosh.* I shushed him, but his eyes were wide with fear. Realizing that Luther wouldn't be getting any quieter, Appleby picked up his cutters and clipped the barbed wire even faster. To give Appleby some protection, I trained my rifle on the German trench. They must have had a bonfire going because I could see sparks trailing up toward the stars. They were probably all warm in their huddle, reading Christmas letters from home. And then the singing started. Although I didn't know much German, I knew the song and what it meant.

Stille Nacht! Heilige Nacht!
Lange schon uns bedacht
Als der Herr vom Grimme befreit,
In der Väter urgrauer Zeit
Aller Welt Schonung verhieß,
Aller Welt Schonung verhieß.

Some sang with a tender, broken longing. Others sang with a drunk, boisterous flair to forget such longing. For an instant, the memory of a long ago Christmastime dragged me away from the cold and the mud and the fear. There I was, all of seven years old, helping Father haul in the tree as he praised me for being so strong. Once it was up, we draped tinsel on the branches, and Mum and Granny made a new wreath to hang on the door. I remembered stomping my foot until Mum marched over to Baker's Sweets to buy my favorite chocolate truffles. I could almost taste them.

Stille Nacht! Heilige Nacht!
Hirten erst kundgemacht
Durch der Engel Alleluja,
Tönt es laut bei Ferne und Nah:
Jesus der Retter ist da!
Jesus der Retter ist da!

The smell of garlic wafted on the smoke from the German trench. They were cooking ... sausage? It sizzled over the embers. Further down the line, in a machine-gun turret, I noticed the pointed tips of those familiar helmets bobbing up and down. Hold on, what were those chaps up to?

All the prattle died and gave way to a terrible, shrieking whistle.

"Shell!"

Appleby sprang to his feet and took off running, right across No Man's Land. The German line lit up with gunfire. The cornered animal sprang to life within me, and I was suddenly dragging Luther toward the nearest crater. My ears popped. My bones rattled. *Blast!* A flash of white, and Mother Earth left me. No pressure of the ground beneath and no sense of the sky above; no up, no down. Tumbling through the air, swept up like a wave on a beach, my body so hot it stung cold. I flailed my arms as if to straighten myself, but to no avail. The world flew by and I flew with it.

I don't know how long I was out, but I woke to searing pain. Yet all I could think of was Luther. *Luther.* I'd made a promise. I said I'd keep him alive. I called his name, but only a croak escaped me. I gathered the Earth in my reddened palms and touched it to my mouth—I don't know why—then pulled myself forward. The world was nothing but blurred slow-motion silhouettes, yet I dragged myself toward him, toward the dark body I knew must be him. *Luther must live. Luther must live. I promised.* I reached out my hand, grabbed hold of the edge of a wet, woolen sweater, and then everything went dark.

My eyes fluttered open, and I stared up at the sky wondering what people would say when they'd see me. A burned husk of a man, poor soul. What would Mum do with me? What would Father say? Soft white snowflakes drifted down from on high, falling on hot skin. I closed my eyes and let them fall.

~ JIM BAKER ~

The train rolled out from the Le Havre station at dawn, squealing and chugging across the French countryside—fenced-in patches of frosty white and dried-up yellow grass that quilted the hills. Occasionally, we'd cross a frozen river. We'd stop for local stations at the intersection of dirt roads where refugees hiked. Occasionally, I locked eyes with the poor souls as we passed. I could not imagine what else they'd seen. What they'd lived through. What had Luther seen? What had he lived through?

I checked my watch. If only this train could chug faster. Fate permitting, I'd be with Luther late tonight or early tomorrow morning. There'd be no sleep for me tonight.

I checked inside my bag to make sure the tickets to Algeria were still there. What would Luther say when he saw me after all these years?

For company, I had Private Roberts, an engineer who had once worked as a mechanic near Manchester. As the assigned guard, he was paid to sit all day in the train car to make sure nobody stole the post. I asked him who would want to steal a soldier's love letter, and he scratched his head.

"A very lonely guard."

I chuckled.

"Well, let me know if you come across one of those. In the meantime, I'm taking a nap." I curled up on top of a couple sacks of mail and let the rattling of the railroad car rock me to sleep. Wearing my coat and extra socks—it was as cozy as being in the womb.

I didn't sleep long, and when I woke I noticed a fine lot of identical cardboard boxes tied with twine and stacked amidst the sacks. Curious. Pulling the twine and opening the flaps, I snuck a look inside one to find it filled with elaborately engraved bronze tins, each the size of my palm. The words CHRISTMAS 1914 were engraved beneath a profile of Princess Mary, surrounded by laurels. *So these must be from the Christmas gift fund Mum got the candy order for.*

Popping the lid off the tin, I saw it packed with cigarettes, a little Christmas card from the Princess herself, and some butterscotch candy—little amber jewels to suck on throughout the day. I chuckled. For all I knew, my own mother made this candy with her bare hands, and here I was, across the sea, holding them in my palm. I closed the tin and put it back in its box.

I shuffled through the post a bit more and found a sack with letters from my neck of the woods. I couldn't resist taking a peek. Probably one in ten of the blokes in Luther's regiment were from near Leamington Spa, and as I sorted through the posts, I saw familiar names, including some from my boarding school in Rugby. While flipping through envelopes, I paused at a letter addressed to *Ethyl Brand*. Ethyl Brand. Reading the name woke a wound in me, like pressing against an old bruise. I picked it up and turned it over. It looked official. Ethyl. Over the years, I had often recalled the times we'd sat by the river together, often wondered where she was and how she was doing. Hadn't seen her since the 1800s. Aunt Lavinia said she'd left Leamington to become a missionary. I lingered on that letter, wondering what was inside. And what was she doing on the front? Oh, I'd better come off it. None of my business. Awful nosy of me to be rifling through these letters in the first place.

"When do you suppose it will snow?" Private Roberts asked, looking out the window at the frosted and shriveled countryside.

"No idea." I shrugged. But I hope it snows soon. I mean, what's Christmas without snow? It's already cold as hell, so we might as well get the precipitation to match." I put Ethyl's letter back in the bag and pulled the drawstring tight.

He nodded and kept his eyes focused on the passing fields. With a long sigh, he rested his head on the windowsill.

"Say, you know where the loo is?" I asked. "Is there a special car for that, or do we just piss off the side?"

"Two cars down."

"Cheers, mate." Gripping the railing, I pulled myself to my feet, leaving the warmth of the car for the balcony outside. The ground rushed past, and I stepped over the coupler linking the two cars. The floor buckled and clanked beneath me, and I stepped into the other car, this one also stuffed full of post. I crossed the car, my bloated bladder coaxing me on. When I reached the other side, my boot landed on something soft. I looked down to see a small doll, a man in a red cloak with a white beard and a bag over his shoulder. Santa Claus. I bent down to pick it up, and before I straightened up, I heard a gasp.

"Est-ce que vous, Pére Noël?"

A tiny, high-pitched voice cut through the dull rattling of the car, followed by a few *shh's*. I could've sworn it sounded like a little girl, like one of the kids who lived down the hall from me in that last boarding house. I could tell by the inflection of the words that she was asking a question, like *Is it you, Pére Noël?* Only I had no idea who Pére Noël was.

"Ce que tu lis? Ce livre—est-il un histoire?"

A shiver rushed up my spine, and goose-pimples skittered across my skin. The stacks of post sacks slanted shadows across the car. Stowaways. Refugees?

If I was a kid, where would I hide?

I stepped forward carefully. After all, if there were kids hiding in here, I didn't want to scare them. I peered behind first one and then another mail sack until I saw her. A shivering little girl crouched there—white-haired with a little round nose, surrounded by dolls and an open suitcase stuffed with more dolls. She said something in French, and then her eyes came to rest on the pistol at my side. She pulled back into herself, obviously wary.

I held my hands up. "It's okay, it's okay. I'm not going to hurt you." Two more girls poked their heads out from behind post sacks. The older one stood, reached into her skirt pocket, and pulled out a nasty, curved knife with a blade a good five inches long. It was an army knife—French, German, or British, I couldn't tell. Once I caught a good look at it, she stowed it back into her skirts.

I realized the littlest one—she was probably about five years old—was staring at the doll in my hand. I held it out to her. "Is this yours?"

She snatched it from me and looked down at the doll and then up at me. "*Pére Noël!*"

"Who?"

"*Pére Noël! Pére Noël!*"

"All right, who is this Pére Noël? Why do you keep calling me that?"

She pointed at me and then eyed the duffel bag slung over my shoulder. I squinted at my reflection in the window—a little bit of my beard had grown back since I had last shaved, and I was tugging a bulging duffel bag over my shoulder. I studied the doll, then my own reflection. The doll. Me. The doll. Me.

"*Pére Noël,*" the little girl said, handing me the doll.

"God, no. Ah, no. Not at all." I shook my head. "I'm no Santa Claus. My name is Jim Baker. *Je suis appelé Jim Baker.*"

"*Non,*" the girl shook her head.

"*Non Pére Noël,*" I corrected her.

I set my bag down to prove it. They gathered 'round me as I undid the buckles and dumped out the contents—a week's worth of clothes, lots of rolled-up socks, toiletries, ammunition, cigarettes, money, and a folder full of my personal documents.

"See," I said. "I've no toys. These are my supplies."

The girls prattled amongst themselves.

"Where are you parents?" I finally asked the oldest girl. She was probably no older than ten. "Your *pére* and *mére*? Where are they?"

"Refugee," was all she said.

What had I just walked into?

"Do you know any English?" I asked.

She nodded. "Some. A neighbor was English." Her eyes glistened and she wiped her nose.

"Alright. What are your names?"

"*Je suis appelé Celeste Moreau,*" she pointed to herself. *Celeste Moreau.*

She nodded at the middle girl. "*Adele Moreau.*"

Then, the smallest sister, who obsessively clung to the Santa doll. "*Bernadette Moreau.*"

"Jim Baker," I pointed at myself.

"*Non,*" Celeste shook her head, "*Pére Noël.*"

"Where are your parents?" I asked them, this time louder.

She shook her head and looked away. I didn't press. She wouldn't talk about her parents just because I shouted.

"Where are you from? Your home?"

"North Pole," Celeste replied.

Suddenly, little Bernadette rushed me, throwing her arms around my waist, her silver-blond hair—frayed and dirty—draped over my arm. I tried thinking of some smart response, some way to scold her for throwing herself at a strange man with a gun. It was dangerous, foolish. But what could I say that she would understand? I stood there, dumb, and for once, I had no smart comeback, no quip to lighten the mood. My heart slowed, my chest loosened, and all of the noise in my head softened and quieted. I looked down to see her burying her face in my shirt, eyes screwed shut, as if I, Santa Claus, had the power to quell her pain. It was one of those moments that slowed time, and the only thought that occurred to me was how gentle, how vulnerable, how hopeful she was. Like a smoldering wick, the slightest breeze would blow her out. So I hugged her back and held my hand against her little head, and imagined this was how fathers felt. *Get a hold of yourself, Jim.*

"Hold on," I croaked out and quickly left the car.

In the back of my mind, I felt a darkness, a fear that I'd done something wrong. I remembered when I was young, at my Aunt Lavinia's wedding, Ethyl Brand had grabbed me by the hands and tried pulling me out onto the dance floor. We were about five, and I was so red with embarrassment that I tore my hands out of hers and hid in the bushes outside. I'd always rejected tenderness like I'd rejected fruitcake—too much sweetness made me sick. That's what I got for growing up in a sweet shop. I thought of Mum and felt that it had something to do with her. Her and Luther. Love him sweet, she always said when trying to keep calm during one of Luther's fits. Love Luther sweet, but give Jim the back of your hand.

Stop being maudlin, Jim!

I nodded at Private Roberts when I returned to the post car. "I'm gonna try to get some real shut-eye in the other car," I said. "Knock first."

He smirked.

Before I stepped back into the other car with the Moreau girls, I took a by-now, much-needed piss off the side and watched the dark countryside roll by. What kind of world was it that made refugees of little girls? What kind of world was it that sent men like Luther to war? No kind I'd ever understand.

Back in the other car, I stacked a couple of postal bags on top of each other and draped my oil cloth coat over them, creating a cozy little fort. Bernadette and Adele crawled inside with their dolls, giggling, while Celeste and I locked eyes. She watched me as I dug at the bottom of my bag and pulled out a tin of figs. I opened it and handed it to her. She pulled out her knife and stabbed one fig each, giving out precious rations to her little sisters, who each received larger portions than her. Then came a tin of peaches. After all of the fruit had been skewered, they took turns passing the tin back and forth to sip the syrup. Celeste wouldn't take any of the syrup and instead left it for the two young ones. Then she offered some to me, but I waved it off, patting my stomach and frowning.

"Too much sweetness makes me sick."

But she insisted, and after a few more attempts to refuse, I tipped the tin back and sucked down the last the last of the sweet syrup, feeling the tiny grains of peach dissolve on my tongue.

"Thank you," I said. She nodded back solemnly as if the transaction was confirmation of a pact made between us.

For most of the rest of the ride, I sat on the floor next to Celeste, backs propped up against a mail sack as we watched Adele and Bernadette play in the fort with their dolls. The more I watched, the more I came to understand the plot of their make-believe story. It all began with a little girl, or several, living and playing happily. Then, a male figure appeared and threw them around. The dolls then escaped and spent a long time wandering and hiding, eventually finding a safe haven with Santa Claus, or *Pére Noël*, where they would live happily ever after. They repeated this plot with many variations, their brows furrowing each time the male doll came to grab them.

"You know, tomorrow is Christmas," I said to Celeste. "Maybe Pére Noël will leave you a gift."

"You must know," she said, "*vous êtes Pére Noël.*"

"I'm not. I'm just Jim, Jim Baker."

I sat there watching the girls for about twenty minutes and then got bored. I pulled out *A Tale of Two Cities* and flipped to the last scene, which I'd read dozens if not hundreds of times. The girls looked up from their dolls when I opened the book. A few minutes later, Adele and Bernadette returned to their play. Celeste kept watching me, though.

"What is the story?" she asked. "*Bien?*"

"It's a good story," I nodded. "It's about, um, well—a man, a good man, gets arrested in France because he is related to the enemy. You understand?"

She nodded.

"So he's a Brit—a very decent, kind Brit—trapped in France, destined to die, and another fellow who's not so decent and kind rescues him."

"Rescues? How?"

"Well, the two men—the good man and the bad man—they are very alike. The bad man wants to redeem himself for the bad things he's done, and he travels all the way from England to France, which is a very dangerous journey. Finally, he finds the good man, who's trapped—"

My throat closed.

"What? What does he do?"

"They switch places." I smiled, forcing myself to keep a straight face. "The bad man dresses up to look like the good man. The good man gets off free, while the bad man is executed in his place. And he tells everyone, 'It is a far, far better thing that I do than I have ever done.'"

"This makes you sad," she noted.

"Oh, I'm not sad," I sniffed. "It's just, I got this book for my brother for his birthday many years ago, but I never gave it to him. That's what I'm doing here. I'm going to give the book to him for real this time."

I doubt Celeste's English was good enough to understand, but she nodded and smiled anyway.

"Your brother is in France? Is he soldier?"

"Something like that."

Around noon, the train slowed and I woke to see Adele and Bernadette curled up inside the fort and realized Celeste was snoring softly, tucked up against my side. Outside, the engineer pulled the breaks, and the train squealed as the wheels rubbed against the steel tracks. Sparks flew, and the train slowed to a stop.

I pulled myself to my feet and gathered my things back into my bag. "I have to go," I said. "I have work to do."

Celeste sat up and tilted her head to look at me. "You go find your brother? To give him the book?"

My brother? It took me a moment to remember I'd told her Luther was in France. What had I been thinking, confiding in a ten-year-old refugee?

"I suggest you clear out quick. Men will come to unload the post. They'll find you."

The girls conversed among each other in French, sounding distressed. *Uh oh.* What if they started crying? What if Roberts the guard came in? What if the police found them and took them away? What would I say? What would happen to them? As a boy, I remembered hearing old man Carraway say that it's best not to butt into the affairs of the disadvantaged unless you know what you're doing. Otherwise, you could just end up hurting them. Like feeding a stray dog. Wow, what a terrible comparison.

But, I couldn't worry about these three girls. There were agencies and refugee centers equipped for that. I had come all this way for Luther. That was it. Period.

APRIL, 1898

LEAMINGTON SPA, ENGLAND

~ THE VILLAGE ~

Dew beaded on streetlamps and darkened cobblestones as the seasonal thaw warmed Leamington Spa. The grey watercolors of spring bled in the sky. *Tap tap tap*, the rain dripped off leaves and pooled into muddy puddles.

Two boys strolled down the dirt road toward Mr. Brand's farm, one clutching a brown paper parcel under his arm. On the tag, his mother had written, *Mr. Brand, here are the Easter chocolates you requested. No need to pay; take it as a gift for your kindness. Sincerely, Constance Baker.*

Mr. Brand had tracked mud across the threshold of Baker's Sweets on Maundy Thursday, before the busy weekend of making hot cross buns and crème eggs and Simnel cakes for Easter festivities.

"I'm putting on a surprise for the family, you see, after church on Easter. It's been a hard winter at the farm and all, and I would have them smile, yes?"

"Yes," Constance nodded without acknowledging the pain in Mr. Brand's eyes. But she had risen early to make the chocolates, box them, tie them with twine, and call

Jim in from playing in the street to make the delivery. As usual, he had dirt on his cheeks.

"You know the Brand's farmhouse?"

"No."

"Yes, you jolly well do. Ethyl's in your grade. They live off Radford Road. Her father and uncle played music at Auntie Lavinia's wedding."

"I said no. I don't know it."

"Lord, Jim, you certainly do know Ethyl. You played together when you were babes."

Jim studied his shoes. "Don't know her," he declared, a bit too loudly and a bit too red faced.

"Fine, fine. Radford Road. Just follow the address."

Jim looked up at his mother. Her eyes narrowed as if daring him to say it.

"But I don't want to. It's started to rain again."

"You were just playing out in the rain, so it's obvious you're not going to melt."

"But—"

"Get going or your face won't just be red from blushing."

As soon as Jim closed the door behind him, jumped down the stoop, and headed down the street, his friend Rodney Stoker stopped kicking his ball around, and fell in beside him.

"Where're you off to?"

"I don't know."

"What's the parcel for?"

"A delivery." Jim stomped in a puddle, and a few commas of mud sprayed up on the hem of his pants—the hem his mother had asked Auntie Lavinia to repair.

"What're you smiling for?"

"I'm just looking at the mud."

They walked in silence a while, and then Jim stopped. "Hey, I got an idea! What do you say we go fishing?" Jim pointed over the stone wall that partitioned the field stretching off from one side of the road. "We're not far from the river."

"Let's do it."

Jim and Rodney jumped the wall and tore over the open farmland until they breached the line of trees drooping over the River Leam. Still under his arm, the box in the brown paper wrapping was now rain-speckled and smashed flat.

And then he saw her. She was there. *Right there.*

The girl. Ethyl Brand. He knew full well who she was. He knew her name. He knew where her desk was in the schoolroom and he knew he had pulled her braids more than once, and, one time, when the schoolmaster asked him to solve an arithmetic problem with her, he'd kicked her. He didn't know why. He shook his head at the memory. *I always mess things up. She shouldn't be kicked. Nobody should ever kick her! She's ... she's what? I don't know. A flower? A bird? An angel?*

And he was supposed to be delivering the parcel of chocolates to her house. To her father. But instead he'd tried to avoid seeing her by going to the river. And now here she was.

His stomach bubbled.

She was barefoot and perched on a sandbar at the river's edge, watching the leaves twist in the current. A tree with white bark drooped its branches over her like an umbrella, and in its branches, a red bird chirped. The whole world was green and grey and brown and damp like wet dirt. But her hair was red, like a fiery halo.

"Maybe Ethyl wants to go fishing, too," Rodney started running, but Jim threw an arm out to stop him.

"I-I," Jim toed the mud while he stuttered. "Let's just leave her be. Looks like she wants to be alone, anyway. We can go fish somewhere else."

"But—" Rodney started to protest, but Jim put his finger to his lips to shush him and then crept forward to set the box of chocolates on the crumbling, old stone wall where Ethyl had set her shoes. Where she was sure to see it. And then he tip-toed away with Rodney, leaving the gift of chocolates behind.

A few days later, Jim arrived at the schoolhouse to find another brown paper parcel on his desk, this time tied with a blue ribbon. *Thank you for the chocolates*, the tag read, *I hope this gift makes you smile.* He could feel Ethyl's eyes trained on him from her desk in the corner, but he didn't dare acknowledge her. When he was sure nobody else had noticed his curling grin, he pulled the ribbon loose, unwrapping the paper. Inside was a book, *A Tale of Two Cities*. For the rest of class that day, in between lessons about multiplication, Jim kept a hand over his mouth to conceal his smile.

Jim spent more time lingering after that, at church, on the country roads, near the river and the like, wondering if he would run into her. She seemed to have a favorite spot to reflect, and that was in the same place he and Rodney had seen her on the banks of the River Leam, under the trees. Taking a deep breath, he finally approached her one day, the book in his hands.

"Hello," he said, and sat down beside her on the sand-bar.

She mumbled a casual, "Evening," as if they spoke that way every day.

"Thanks for the book," he said. He picked up a stick and started drawing shapes in the sand. "I've actually read this one before. You see, my dad had a lot of Charles Dickens books he left for me after he died. I've read them all. I didn't understand most of the words and don't remember what happened, but I read them. There's *A Tale of Two Cities, Great Expectations, A Christmas Carol.*"

"Which is your favorite?" Ethyl asked. She started drawing in the sand, too.

"*A Christmas Carol.* It's an awful sad story, but at the same time a most happy story. I like Christmas stories."

Ethyl turned to look at him. "Those are good reasons."

"Would you like to meet here tomorrow and talk some more?" Jim blurted, heart racing. He thought it was probably asking too much of her, especially since this one conversation had taken a week to cultivate.

"I would," she whispered before standing up and sprinting back toward her farm.

Jim watched her until she disappeared and then looked down to see a heart drawn in the sand.

~ JIM BAKER ~

Mum stopped going to church after the time Luther threw a prayer book and hit an old lady in the back of the head. The priest came to our door that afternoon and said Luther might have a demon inside him, and Mum shut the door in his face. Still she made me go every weekend with Auntie Lavinia and Uncle Mark.

Especially on Easter.

Today Father Carmichael spoke from the pulpit behind the gate with his gentle, old-man voice that echoed through the pillared cavern. His words were careful and spread out all soft and droopy, like icing on a cake.

"We began this year of Our Lord in darkness, during the winter when nights were long. That was when the Lord came to the Earth, not as a militant king in flowing vestment, but as a humble babe …"

He paused especially long, so long that everyone in the pews could think about the importance of Jesus as a humble baby. My attention wandered to the ceiling, and I imagined, like I always did, that I was Jonah and the church was a whale, swallowing me up. And then there was the kaleidoscope window that I always thought looked like a giraffe was hiding in it.

At one point, Father Carmichael started talking about parenthood, and I had no idea why. "Let us start at birth," he said, "when the love between parents is so great that it creates life. When that child is born, its parents shower it with love and wait on it every hour of the day, oftentimes going without sleep. I cannot name a mother who would rather live in comfort while her child suffers."

I could think of one.

A hand spread out on my back, and I shivered. I looked up to see Auntie Lavinia smile and pull me close into her side. She had freckles and black hair, just like me. She smelled like flowers, and I hugged her back, but just for a second so nobody saw. Uncle Mark looked over and winked at me. I liked him okay. He had kind eyes set in a thin face adorned with a meager mustache.

I smiled back and then looked over at Ethyl and her family. They always sat in the pew across from us. I stole a glance at her and she turned and looked at me. I could feel my cheeks redden. Luckily, the adults picked up the hymn books, turned to the page, and started singing. I looked at Auntie Lavinia's book and sang the words from it.

Now the green blade riseth from the buried grain,
Wheat that in the dark earth many days has lain;
Love lives again, that with the dead has been:
Love is come again, like wheat that springeth green.

The bells *bong bong bonged*, and Auntie Lavinia had to stop me from running down the aisle and out into the square, where I knew the Easter Egg hunt would soon begin. I'd never been allowed to stay for the hunt because Mum didn't think it was fair to Luther. Because of course Luther couldn't hunt eggs. Luther couldn't do much of anything.

"Can I do the hunt this year, Auntie Lavinia? Please?"

"Let's go home and ask your mother, love. Maybe this year will be different."

Dammit. I marched back home with Auntie Lavinia and Uncle Mark holding hands. Meanwhile, the men with the mustaches and top hats gathered up all the kids in front of church. They were kids like Farmer Brand's goats were kids, all rounded up and bleating in a circle, patches of tweed and cotton and black shoes that their mothers had tied too tight and they cried over all morning. The fat man in the top hat and mustache told the rules that I already knew and then raised his flag—a white table cloth—and flashed it twice to signal the contest. The kids radiated outward, giggling, gossiping, peeking under every flower pot and inside every bird house. One of them pulled out a blue, penny-sized egg from the bird house and put it in their pocket. *That's a robin egg, not an Easter Egg.* One of the adults made the little girl put it back.

"If Luther can't join the Easter Egg hunt, then neither can you," Mum said once I got home. "It's not fair for him to watch you go have fun while he can't. So, I'm sorry, but the answer is no."

"But Mum, *please*. It's Easter. And he's here, not out there watching."

Behind her, I watched the cupboard door in the kitchen open on its own. Out rose Luther, yawning, making those squeaky rubbery noises to himself. How long had he been asleep in the cupboard? As he stretched and rubbed his eyes, I thought of the verses from the hymn we had sung at church.

Forth he came at Easter, like the risen grain,
He that for three days in the grave had lain;
Quick from the dead my risen Lord is seen:
Love is come again, like wheat that springeth green.

Mum locked her gaze on me, and that same feeling passed between us that always passes between us. Usually at this point, if I said one more word, I'd get slapped or hit with a ruler. But Mum's brow did not harden. She looked at Luther and then back at me and then at Auntie Lavinia, and then she sighed and started to untie her apron.

"Fine, yes. I'll take Luther on his first Easter Egg hunt today. You go on and find your friends."

The townsfolk had done an Easter Egg hunt in Leamington Spa every year since always. The kids would search for eggs, and the adults would eat cucumber sandwiches and look at the kids looking. Whoever found the most eggs by noon won a prize, a little metal plaque that Rodney told me was made of gold. *Rodney ... I wonder where he is ...* Wait! He would probably be good at finding eggs, and the two of us could win and walk up to the pavilion at noon with shirtfulls of eggs and get the plaque. Those other kids who sniveled and hid behind their fathers when me and Luther went around, who stole my pants and called my mother names, who made me eat dirt and gave me whoopings, they needed to be beaten and beaten good.

I found Rodney next to a tent set up in the greenspace by the river, where men drank scotch and smoked cigars and said dammit and hell. Rodney was sitting next to the tent cloth, knees folded up, chopping a stick into pieces with his dad's knife.

He nodded at me, then put a finger to his lips.

"Hey," I whispered. "The Easter Egg hunt started already. Wanna make a team and find them all before the other kids?"

"Jim, do you ever wish you were in the army?"

"What?"

"There's some older boys—Tom Jansen and Michael Pinckney—smoking cigars and talking about how they joined the army. They're in the tent right now."

Rodney pointed his thumb at the rippling cloth wall beside him.

"Where did they fight?"

"Sounds like South Africa."

The men in the tent started laughing, and Rodney pressed a finger to his lips and an ear to the tent.

I heard clinking glasses and lots of coughing, and Rodney tried to breathe in the smoke from the cigars. And then I heard the voices.

"You should've seen the savages, running naked and pillaging indiscriminately. Elephants running wild—ivory on legs, we called them. Nasty place. Know how to hold you own there, and you're a rich man, though."

Savage? What makes someone savage? I wanted to ask because when I knocked over old Mrs. Highsmith's beehive, she called me a savage and my mum gave me a whupping she said was fit for a savage. I didn't ask though. I just crouched down next to the flapping tent cloth that stunk of cigar.

"There was a man in our regiment who was caught trying to flee from the action. He dropped his gun and ran for the nearest village. Military police found him, tried him in court for cowardice, was found guilty of desertion, and executed about a month later."

"Come on, Rodney, I don't like this." I pulled on the collar of his Sunday best. "Let's look for the eggs now."

But Rodney's eyes were wide and empty because his thoughts were in South Africa.

"I've held my dad's gun before, you know. He let me."

I got the feeling that the British soldiers in South Africa would have looked into his empty eyes all day if not for the sudden bustle and clinking of glass inside the tent.

"Ch—Charles dear, we were going over to the Masons' for lunch, remember?"

Rodney's mum. We could tell she'd ventured inside the tent unwelcome because as soon as she spoke, all the coughing and grumbling and swearing died down, and the young men went quiet when they found a lady in their midst.

"Five, Margaret. Me and Fred Mason spoke. They wanted us over at five."

"Sorry, but why would Fred Mason host a lunch at five in the afternoon? Come on, now, please."

Rodney's dad was silent. Nobody laughed at his mistake, either. Except for me, that is. Pressing a hand over my mouth to hide my giggles, I leaned my ear up against the tent cloth, along with Rodney. We heard a sound of swishing fabric—maybe Rodney's dad was putting on his coat, maybe he was laying down his napkin on the table, or maybe even wiping his sweaty forehead.

"Pardon me," a different voice spoke up to break the tension, "eh—"

"Call me Mrs. Stoker."

"Very well, Mrs. Stoker. I'm new to Leamington, just finished serving in Africa, and I'm trying to learn the names. There's a woman who runs the sweet shop. I gather you're friends?"

Rodney and I met eyes, and I felt my chest tighten. Whoever this man was, his voice was swelled and puffy like a balloon. He sounded like my Uncle Peter. Uncle Peter gets sick when he drinks too much, and in the evenings, his voice swells up just like that, like when I spent the holiday at his farm over in Rugby.

"Are you referring to Constance Baker? No, I do not make a habit of socializing with her."

Without thinking, I tore up a chunk of grass from the ground and made sure that Rodney could see me. I made a mental note to put snails or grubs or something slimy in his mum's handbag.

"I guess what I'm trying to get at is," the man's voice continued to swell until he was talking over himself, "this Constance Baker, she seems a fine woman, fine and put together and pious. I gather there's no Mr. Baker?"

Rodney's face got red, and he shifted on his hams, crossing his arms. I scratched my head with ferocity. *I'm leaving, right now.* But I didn't.

"Cut the nonsense, Tom." another man spoke up, "That's the whiskey talking. You wouldn't want to court Mrs. Baker."

"Why not? I ask again—is there a Mr. Baker?"

"No," I peeked under the tent wall to see Rodney's mum study the dirt beneath her feet. "Not anymore," she said.

I swallowed.

"Sad," Rodney's dad spoke up, "It's a hard thing, having a house without a father. Not good for the children. That Jim Baker especially. Call me a fool if he doesn't end up with his head cracked open one day."

"Boys like Jim Baker are no enigma, love," Rodney's mum said. "If you won't breed a sheepdog with a tramp, then don't breed a gentleman with a, a…"

My hands shook, and I got that feeling I usually got right before I try and fight one of the older boys always making fun of Luther. But now they were making fun Mum. I peeked under the tent to see Mrs. Stoker's face scrunch up like her tea had turned to vinegar.

"Have you met Mrs. Baker?" she asked the newcomer. "It'd be a meeting you'd never forget."

"Indeed?" the same man said. "Tell me."

"You've seen how she paints her face. It's ghastly. Red lips, dark eyes, I can't tolerate it. I heard from my cousin that she's, well, a loose woman."

Mr. Stoker coughed. "Who told you that?"

"Maisie—you know, Maisie Collins."

"Maybe Maisie's right, or maybe she's just a busybody. I wouldn't trust that woman to make my toast, and you shouldn't be spreading gossip."

"Yet you trust me to make your dinner."

A puff of laughter filled the tent, and Mr. Stoker swallowed his whiskey before losing his solemn, rotisserie composure. He motioned his glass toward himself.

"No wonder the Baker boys are so ..." Mrs. Stoker went on.

"I don't think that's fair," Mr. Stoker said. "You know Luther can't help the way he is. And Jim's not a bad sort. Good friend to our boy, remember."

"These things are inherited, and the mother seems plenty strange to me," Mrs. Stoker said, straightening up like she was going to give a lecture. "Why one time, when I was in the store, Rodney and I saw Luther have one of his fits. It was a sight I shan't soon forget."

To hell with it. With them all. I dropped the edge of the tent and stood up to go, hands clenched, jaw set, when I noticed the rock Rodney was crouched on a tiny ivory shine in the grass.

"Rod—an egg! You've been sitting on it this whole time, you chicken!"

Rodney snatched the egg up and stuck it in his trouser pocket. Finally, I dragged him away from the tent, and within a few minutes, we were searching for eggs and having fun. Kind of.

Whoever hid the Easter eggs had a ruddy go of it because we found them all over—in birdbaths, bushes, windowsills, some even just lying in the grass where people could step on them. They were painted eggs, too, dipped in blue and green pulpy water in coffee cups in the kitchen like Mum used to. Mum.

I heard her coming before I saw her.

"Look, Luther, there's the egg. See? No, Luther, right there—see? In the flower pot. The flower pot. Luther, look at me. Go to the flower pot."

"Ba," it took him so much effort to say that. He pressed his lips hard and thought deep for the syllables. The sounds came out shrill, like an out-of-tune instrument, and he clung onto Mum to hide from all the other faces staring at him, blubbering in her shoulder.

"Luther, *no sounds. Use words.* The flower pot, Luther."

She sounded just as happy as she always did around Luther. I imagined she was telling herself over and over again to *love him sweet*. The thought made me sick to my stomach.

"Ba."

Luther was just about as tall as Mum now, which made the other kids stop and gape when they heard his sounds. They got quiet like they always did and shrank behind their parents. They were all afraid of him. Pricks.

Mum and Luther were coming around the corner, and I didn't want to be there when they arrived. I was standing on Rodney's hands because he was giving me a boost to see over Mrs. Robert's garden wall. I didn't see any eggs, but there was a big plate of golden-sweet hot cross buns cooling on the table on her veranda and a street cat circling the table and rubbing its neck on them. *Mmm.* My arms shook as I pulled myself over the wall and into the yard, where I opened the gate for Rodney to come in. We tip-toed over the gravel, and the cat stared at us. It started walking in figure eights around the tabletop, restless as we approached.

I heard that rubber-squeaking sound, the constant sound of someone inhaling in delight. Luther stumbled through the gate on his toes, flapping his hands and jumping when he saw the cat. He ran right past us, not even noticing the dozen painted eggs Rodney and I were holding in our shirts. The cat's eyes widened into saucers; it arched its back, twitched its tail, and darted off the table and into the bushes.

When Luther saw me, he ran up and hugged me, but I kind of pushed him away because I didn't want Rodney to see us hugging. But then Luther did the same thing to Rodney, and Rodney gave Luther a shove, too.

So I hit Rodney. What's a brother to do? Sometimes I don't even know why I lash out, but as soon as I'd done it, I knew I shouldn't have. Luther froze up like he does sometimes, his face all blank.

"Luther? Luther where are you?" I heard Mum's voice in the background.

Rod crouched over, covered his face, and got real quiet. I thought he was going to start crying and get us all in trouble. *Come on, Rodney, don't be a baby.* He stayed crouched. *Rodney ...*

I inched over and touched Rod's back to see what he'd do, and he got up and smashed all his eggs on my shirt, giggling. They were all boiled, of course, and left yellow grainy marks like dry boogies. But he ruined my Sunday's best. *Whew.* We were going to be okay.

I laughed. "Want me to do you?"

He nodded, and I smashed all my eggs on his shirt. There were a thousand tiny *crack crack cracks,* and he had white and yellow egg flesh all over his suit, a few pieces of shell still sticking on. The both of us stood there giggling. I reached out and poked his shoulder, and he had the same idea. Next second, we were both pretending to be tough guys. I sent my fist at him in slow motion, and he grabbed it and pretended to twist it. I went along with him, flopping on the gravel of Mrs. Robert's garden, clutching my arm and seething.

"Where's the money?" Rod stood over me.

"I buried it, wise guy."

"Aw, yeah?"

"Yeah. You'll never get your dirty hands on it now!"

Rodney suddenly got distracted and reached over to snatch one of the hot cross buns that Mrs. Roberts had set out to cool. They looked good, so I got up and figured I'd take one, too. Rod was going to take a bite, but there was a fly sitting on it, right on the warm, crisp crust. Rod pulled his finger back to flick the fly off, but it saw him coming and buzzed away.

"Aw man. Looks like I'll have to get that fly another day. Fight's over."

"No hit Jim!"

Oh God. Luther. I'd almost forgot he was still there. Now, he was suddenly screeching and flapping his hands against Rodney. Rodney stuffed a big bite of bun in his mouth and stepped aside. He didn't even try to block Luther. He just turned way. And then he was on the ground, head cracked open on the pavement, and Luther was standing over him.

The fly buzzed back and landed in the pooling blood.

~ CONSTANCE BAKER ~

God in heaven, I had never seen so much blood—staining the skin like ink on paper, darkening the pavement. Luther ran behind me, crouched down on his heels and rocked back and forth while flapping his hands and smacking himself in the head. Jim just stood there. Frozen. Looking down at his friend like he'd never seen him before. For a moment, I stood frozen as well. So much blood—my fingers tingled and my stomach lurched.

I didn't know how to act. I couldn't swallow; I couldn't speak. Maybe someone else, a doctor, would come strolling by, cry out, and seize the body in his arms? He would rush off to the hospital, leaving me just a bystander featured in next week's post. Scenarios dreamed themselves up separate from my thoughts, kind of like how they say life flashes before the dying, one of whom was bleeding out on the ground at my feet. Finally, after what seemed ages but was probably seconds, I bent over Rodney Stoker and lifted his head; my fingers came away sticky with thick blood from the gushing patch at the back of his head.

A bandage? I looked up at Jim and considered pulling his shirt off to use as a bandage, but he might resist and delay me. So I reached for the buttons of my own blouse, pulling it open, yanking it off my shoulders and using the long sleeves to tie it tight it around Rodney's head. The white cotton—the blouse I had borrowed from Lavinia all those years ago and then "forgot" to return was already stained like the strawberries I would coat in chocolate for St. Valentine's Day.

And the blood kept gushing.

I needed to call for help, but my voice wouldn't work. And, besides, we were too far from the village green and there was too much activity for anyone to hear me. Could I carry him? Was that allowed? My arms were jelly, and I feared any touch would break him. I touched his face, no movement. I slid my arms under his knees and his back, and then struggled to stand. He was limp and warm and heavy in my arms.

Where to? The hospital? Too long of a walk—I didn't know how long he even had. Doc Abbott's place on the other side of town? I'd walk up to drawn curtains and a closed gate. The church? I hadn't been there since the in-cident with Luther and the hymnal and the old woman. Besides, as soon as anyone saw me with a bloodied boy, everyone would accuse Luther, no doubt. Especially Mrs. Stoker. Oh, god. What would Mrs. Stoker say?

But the boy needed help. Now. Someone at the Easter festivities would know what to do.

I turned to Jim. "Take Luther home. Now."

Jim looked up at me, shock written on his face.

"Jim!" I wanted to shake him. "Do you hear me? Take your brother home *now*!"

I left my boys and hurried down the cobblestone with Rodney bouncing in my arms, down Gordon Street, around the corner, under the trees, red brick at one side, white plaster on the other. Down the row of vine-curled steel fences where the stray cats hissed as I passed. New Street. Church Terrace. There, ahead, the green at the flank of All Saint's Church where tents flapped and children played chatter buzzed. I saw children running with bubble wands and playing jump rope, fine gentlemen and farmers stumbling down the egg-and-spoon race while their best girls clapped and squealed, prize-winning rabbits with blue ribbons pinned on their cages, and bearded men spinning war stories and sipping on Scotch.

"Doc Abbott! You—where's Doc Abbott?"

I singled out a raggedy old man because raggedy old men seemed to be the only ones who would acknowledge me.

He pulled off his cap and ran. Mothers grabbed their children by the shoulders, covering their eyes and turning them away. A bearded man from one of the tents hurried toward me. He opened his arms and motioned for me to hand over the boy, which I did.

"What happened?"

"Hit his head on pavement—playing like boys do. An accident, a terrible accident."

"We'll get him to the Doctor. Don't you worry yourself. Best tell Mr. and Mrs. Stoker," and the man rushed off with Rodney limp in his arms.

With the warmth of the boy's body gone, the humid air was cold against my skin. I looked down to see my arms were bare and remembered I'd taken off my shirt to staunch the blood. Now, I was standing out in the open in my silk shift, matted and bloody. Young boys stared and then looked away, embarrassed. Some of the women scowled, while others mouthed, *Dear me."*

On the church steps I saw Father Carmichael chatting with a wealthy widow who stopped, put her hand over her mouth and pointed at me. The priest clicked his polished shoes down the front steps, and hurried straight at me. I crossed my arms tight over my chest and held my chin high. People stared as he ripped off his black jacket and draped it over my shoulders.

"Come," he motioned me to walk with him, "It'll do no good having a whole town frown on you."

"What happened?"

"A playful tussle. Jim and Rodney. Rodney took a misstep and tripped." My hand instinctively touched the back of my head. "There was so much blood."

"Who has the boy?"

"I don't know his name. I think he's new in town. He grabbed him and said he'd take him to Doc Abbott's."

"My good people, the crisis is resolved." Father Carmichael's voice echoed over the greenspace as he hurried me along. "Enjoy this holy day in Christ and do not trouble yourselves."

The mothers ushered their children back to their business, but the festivities had lost their vibrance.

"I trust you will accompany me to Doctor Abbott's?"

"What?"

"For the boy's parents—Mr. and Mrs. Stoker, God bless them. They will be frantic, in need of counsel and comforting. You are close with them, are you not?"

"I wouldn't say that."

"You saved their boy's life, Mrs. Baker. And your Jim plays with him all the time—a best pal of Rodney Stoker if I ever saw one. It would be most kind if you explain to them what happened."

"Father, I really don't think they would appreciate—"

"Maybe you could say a prayer with them. For safekeeping of the boy."

"I—I'll do my best."

He set off at a brisk walk down Bath Street, and I tried to keep his pace. I noticed, as we walked, dark drop marks spotting the cobblestone, some connected by a dark drizzle.

"Somebody will have to clean that blood sooner or later," Father Carmichael said. "Let's hope for a nice cool rain to wash our filth away."

I agreed.

The tidy rows of houses stared quietly as we passed under the train bridge. Water dripped on us and a few puddles had settled into the cracks and depressions in the sunken sidewalks next to dented rubbish bins. On the other side of the bridge, Leamington was much less tidy. Everyone said Doc Abbott kept house and office there because that's where the need was greatest. I had been there several times when the boys were young, but had stopped going when the doctor suggested Luther be sent away.

We stopped at a knicked-up white plaster home facing the butcher shop. The plaque out front read:

Abraham Abbott, M.D.
Private Practice

Father Carmichael rapped on the front door several times and then opened the door and motioned me in. Rodney's parents—Margie, who had called Luther a cow and Mr. Stoker, the fat lawyer who always looked me up and down as if I were a piece of meat in the butcher's shop—sat on chairs by the window, both sniffling into handkerchiefs. The waiting room smelled like old furniture, like the musty antique wardrobe of my mother's that Lavinia kept in her bedroom. The curtains were dark, and the outside light peeked through in grey, slanting beams. An empty desk sat in the corner next to the door to the doctor's examining room. The lamps were dusty and gave off little light. I got the impression the doctor was counting on the office being closed on Easter Day.

"Ah, Mr. and Mrs. Stoker," Father Carmichael said, his voice soft and low. "I came as soon as I heard."

Mr. Stoker stood, tall and rigid like he was on an inspection line in the army. He took Father Carmichael's outstretched hand and gripped it tight.

"Stay strong, Charles," Father Carmichael whispered. "Christ is suffering with you."

Mr. Stoker swallowed and blinked back tears. "Thank you, Father. Your presence is a comfort."

"You may have heard, but Mrs. Baker was the one who rescued your son. To ease your hearts, I have brought her along to inform you how your son came to be injured. Mrs. Baker, if you will?"

I couldn't speak. I glanced at Father Carmichael, and he nodded for me to carry on.

I swallowed hard. "It—it was an accident, you see. Jim and Rodney, making horseplay like boys do … they were play-fighting in a garden, and I happened to hear them as I was walking along. I found Rodney had fallen and knocked his head on the pavement. They were just playing, roughhousing. It was Jim. Jim pushed him. I'm so sorry. It was an accident."

The Stoker's eyes met.

"Please, if there is any reparation I can make—"

"You owe us nothing," Mr. Stoker raised a hand to shush me and sunk back into his chair. "If it was an accident, like you say, then we thank you for helping our boy." Stoker looked at me, his eyes hard as pebbles. "A terrible, terrible accident."

"This is the wisest course, Charles." Father Carmichael pulled up another chair and sat down beside him. "Accidents are accidents. This was no plan of God, nor a work of fate. No soul was responsible."

That was when Margie raised her daft pink face, stained with tears and looked straight at me. "Who was watching Luther when you found our boy?"

My throat closed.

"Please," Mr. Stoker smoothed his wife's hair, "it needn't be discussed. There was no ill intent."

"Who was watching Luther?" she repeated.

When a priest and a lawyer walk into a waiting room, they must not be kept waiting, I thought. *I have to say something. I have to say something.* "I, well, he was at my sister Lavinia's house for the day."

Even as I spun the lie, I knew I couldn't make up enough background information to support it. I didn't even know where Lavinia was. She may not even be home, and my story could be proven false at any moment.

"And you only saw Rodney after he fell?" Margie said.

"Yes."

"But you think it was just roughhousing."

I tilted my head to hide my quivering lip and tried to smile at her. "What else could it be? Jim was beside himself. You know as well as I do what great friends they are."

Mr. Stoker leaned forward in his seat, and Father Carmichael raised an eyebrows at me.

Bollocks. Bollocks. Theyknowtheyknowtheyknow!

Then the door to the doctor's office opened, and Dr. Abbott stepped into the waiting room. He pulled off a pair of bloody gloves, wiped the sweat from his brow with a sleeve, and announced that Rodney would most likely recover and be just fine. We all rejoiced, and Margie even gave me a hug. Then I slipped outside, walked down the street until I could disappear into an alley, and fell apart. *They'll know. Rodney will wake up, and he'll tell them what Luther did. Oh God, he'll tell and they'll come get Luther and take him away.*

There would be an assault charge, a conviction, a court-issued sentence to life in a mental asylum. I'd knew about the electroshock therapy and ice baths. I'd seen the men who'd been lobotomized and put in straight jackets, pumped full of drugs. Their eyes. I could never forget their empty eyes. What God would be so sick, what universe so contradictory, as to take away someone's humanity? *My Luther is such a kind boy. He gives hugs and kisses like a baby and hides in cupboards. He wants to hug his mum and brother and give us kisses and hold our hands. Only a heartless bastard would want to change my boy.*

I kicked the rubbish bin and slumped against the wall. Then I stood up and wiped my eyes. *I have to get home. I have to be home for Luther. For when they come to get him.*

Slipping in the back door, I found Lavinia sitting at the kitchen table, sipping a cup of tea. The house was almost as much hers as mine for the amount of time she'd spent there with me and the boys after James died and before she married Mark. She could help herself to whatever she wanted.

She stood and opened her arms, and I fell in them. My little sister. I breathed in deep, so deep as to fill my whole lungs, so I'd stop trembling. Then I exhaled sharply, completely emptying them. In again, out again to calm myself so the boys—who I knew were awake with ears pressed to their doors—couldn't hear me cry.

"Jim told me," Lavinia said. "I was just headed back to the green when I ran into the boys. I brought them home immediately."

"You ... you know what Luther did?"

"Constance, it never happened. Look at me. You told me about the sanitarium and we both know what they'll do to him if the authorities find out and send him there. So, it never happened. It was an accident. Jim did it."

After James died, I was left with two sons and a candy store to run. Plus my father had died recently and my mother had basically disowned me because I'd married without her permission. I was lost. I'd left my whole family behind to come to Leamington Spa to live with my husband and help in his store. We were in love. Luther's birth was a happy affair, and we thought the whole world was good. But then Luther stopped developing like the other children. I asked the local housewives, who said the disease came from promiscuity on the mother's part. Then I asked the priest, who said the disease came from Satan. The doctors told me the mineral springs in Leamington Spa would do the trick—that they'd fix my son. And when that failed, I went to the fortune tellers, the mystics living by the road, and they stole my money.

And then little Jim was born, and we saw a new chance for hope in the world. Then came the accident. With my husband gone, the store to run, and two boys to manage, I wanted to give up.

I used to be gentle, soft, and filled with love, but I became hard, resentful, and filled with hate. I cursed my life and my God. I woke up every day with a tight chest and a clenched jaw, . No amount of sleeping syrup could relieve the stress, no matter how sick it made me. That's what it was—a sickness. Every day I was sick and bitter and broken. My blood boiled in my veins and anger radiated from my pores.

I used to have a different kind of life, one in which I had the luxury to think about books and ideas and politics and philosophy and the future. But that life died and all I could think about was Luther. Because Jim could get along on his own, Luther became my whole existence. All I could do was feed him and try to show him I loved him. Half the time, I knew he was completely oblivious to me, but I kept trying to get through. I couldn't bring myself to give up. Until I couldn't go on anymore. When I confided in a letter to my little sister that I thought the boys would be better without me, she packed her bags and came to live with us. She saved my life.

Lavinia lived with us for two years. She helped me develop a routine that made living with Luther and Jim possible and helped me figure out how to run the store. Then she fell in love with a good man. A man she deserved and that deserved her. She had the life I once had, and I would do anything to see her keep it, just to watch and marvel at what could have been.

And sitting in my kitchen on that horrible day, she saved me again. She hugged me, made me tea, and shushed my sobs.

"Rodney will wake tomorrow," I said finally. "He'll tell everyone what happened. You know Mr. Stoker's the best lawyer in the shire. He'll put Luther away if it's the last thing he does."

"If it comes to that, we'll have to convince him not to. That's all. Mark will talk to him, don't worry. For now, you just get rest. Do you want me to stay the night?"

"No, I'll manage. I always do."

She kissed my forehead, pulled on her sweater, and slipped quietly out back door into the night, and I, for a while, remained at the table and tried to make sense of my chaotic thoughts.

Tick. Tock. Tick. Tock.

The clock on the mantle, surrounded by knick-knacks from a past life—china plates, enameled saucers Granny gave me on my wedding day, marked the time. I roused myself and went into the living room. So many reminders of James and the life we'd been building. His books had pride of place in a lovely bookshelf he'd made himself. We had Malory, Browning, Spencer, Chaucer, and a graphite rubbing of Lord Byron's headstone from Westminister Abbey, where we'd taken our honeymoon. James had collected the complete set of Charles Dickens, acquired book by book throughout the years. The space reserved for *A Tale of Two Cities* was empty now, probably because Jim was reading it in his bed. Whenever there was a crisis, that's what little Jim did. He buried himself in a story, hiding under his covers to block out Luther's screeching. Eyes closed, and I could smell the graphite of the Byron rubbing and pretend I was back James's arms.

Tick. Tock. Tick. Tock.

The clock kept moving; its gears kept turning. Past eleven, past midnight. I paced through the shop, examining the chocolates, taffies, and bonbons that had taken me so many hours to make. Everything seemed so alien and unfamiliar.

Someone rapped softly on the shop door, and I turned to see a face through the glass.

Mr. Stoker.

Our eyes met. It was too late to go upstairs because he had already seen me. I turned the knob and opened the door, but he did not cross the threshold. I realized I was still wearing Father Carmichael's jacket. I stared at him, not sure how I should be feeling. Dawn was hours away, but Rodney could wake at any moment—maybe he was already awake. Maybe he had already told. Maybe that's why Mr. Stoker was here. But no, he didn't know. I could see it in his face. His heart was still open, still soft, still vulnerable and bleeding. This was my only chance to convince him. I had saved his son. Now I needed to save mine.

"Come in." I motioned him in, and he took off his hat.

"I just came back from Doctor Abbot's." He stared at the ground, wringing his hat in his hands. "I sat over Rodney's bed all evening, changing his bandages, watching the bleeding finally stop. It will be some time before he is fit again, but Abbot thinks he will likely recover completely. I thought you would want to know."

"That's wonderful. Has he stirred?"

"Yes. His eyes opened, and I spoke to him."

Tick. Tock. Tick. Tock.

The clock carried on. A quarter to one.

"W—what did he say?"

"His voice was too weak to speak, so he only mouthed words, which I could not make out. But I made it clear to him that he is in good hands and has nothing to worry about."

"I'm so glad to hear it."

Something moved inside me, a dread I had never felt before, a directive that made me sick. The situation was already too far gone for me to look back. If I didn't act now, it would be too late.

"Mr. Stoker, you look exhausted. I have some tea prepared, if you would have it."

"No, I mustn't stay long. Margie is waiting for me."

"Please. It's the least I can do, considering. I will feel terrible unless I can offer something more. After all, it's the moral and ethical thing to comfort our neighbors."

Mr. Stoker puffed out his ample chest and stood tall, shoulders back. His wife had always treated me as if I were a leper, but the very important Mr. Stoker had rarely had anything to do with me at all. And now he was here in my house. In the middle of the night. How odd.

"Well, I guess I should, if only to ease your own considerable pain, Mrs. Baker. So yes, I will accept your offer and share some tea with you."

So that was his prime motivator—morality. Ethics. Being the pillar of the community who always puffs out his chest and declares his intent to do the right thing for God and King. Take that away, and he'd be lost. Vulnerable. *Susceptible.*

Tick. Tock. Tick. Tock.

I led him into the living room, where he sat on the sofa. Then, going into the kitchen, I poured the tea. The kettle was still on the stove and the water still hot. I took a key out of the pocket of my skirt and unlocked the padlock on the medicine cupboard above the stove. Hands trembling,

I pulled out the cork to Luther's sleeping syrup, which I sometimes gave him when he had fits in the night. I let it *drip drip drip* into Mr. Stoker's tea, enough to knock him out for at least an hour or two, along with ample honey and a squeeze of lemon to disguise the taste. I took a deep breath and set his cup on the saucer.

Tick. Tock. Tick. Tock.

Ten till one. I swallowed and made the sign of the cross. *Oh God, will I ever be forgiven for this?* It didn't matter. It didn't matter if I burned in hell, so long as Luther was not locked away in the asylum.

"Here we are," I said, walking out into the living room. I handed him the cup and saucer and sat next to him, so close our thighs touched.

He took a sip and paused. "Thank you," he said. He looked around the room, then back at me. He took another sip as the silence stretched between us. I could see the pallor of worry on his skin. I'm sure he could see the same on mine.

"Mrs. Baker," he began, "I only intended to stop by briefly to tell you that—"

"Yes?"

He stared blankly at the empty space in front of his eyes, forgetting for a moment what he was going to say. He took another sip. And then another as if to fill the awkward silence. He stared at my leg touching his and cleared his throat. His eyes began to travel slowly upward until he caught himself. "I—I was going to establish that there are no hard feelings between our families. I was a boy myself once and know how boys roughhouse. I do not blame Jim for hurting Rodney, so there is nothing to forgive. Nothing for you to worry over."

"If only that were true."

"What?"

"You know, this isn't my jacket. Father Carmichael gave it to me. Could you give it back to him for me?" I pulled off the jacket, revealing my silk slip and bare arms, both stained with his son's blood.

"Why, I—" Mr. Stoker's eyes dropped down to my bosom and then slowly moved back up to my face. His eyes drooped as he fought to stay awake. He shook his head as if to clear it, then slapped his cheek and yawned. "Mrs. Baker ... what I mean is ... what I mean to say ... what is wrong with ... Did you put something in this?"

His words were muddled and the cup and saucer slipped out of his hand and fell to the floor, spilling their contents on the rug. He stared at it for a long moment, and then looked up at me, eyes unfocused.

I wanted to beg his forgiveness, but that would not have accomplished anything. I had to be cold, as cold and hard as necessary. And I had to make sure that this man would never be an obstacle to my son's wellbeing.

"Luther was the one who pushed your son, Mr. Stoker. "Rodney and Jim were roughhousing, but Luther didn't understand. He thought Rodney was truly hurting Jim and so he pushed him. He didn't mean for him to get hurt, but it was Luther. Not Jim. It wasn't just two friends roughhousing."

Mr. Stoker's eyes went wide. "What are you saying?" He tried to stand.

"I'm saying that if Rodney wakes up and remembers what happened, that if the truth comes out and you think to take legal action against my son, I'll tell everyone."

He pushed himself to his feet, wobbled, and grabbed the lampstand to steady himself. "Tell everyone what?"

"That you came here in the middle of the night to take advantage of a defenseless widow."

"But I never—" His words were slurred, and before he could take two steps, he fell to his knees, pulling the lamp down with him. He looked up at me one last time and collapsed on the rug, snoring.

Bong.

The clock struck one o'clock.

~ THE VILLAGE ~

In the quiet moments just before dawn, when the first rays of warmth broke through pink-feather clouds hanging over Bath Street, a fat man stumbled down the cobblestone, holding his tweed cap tight to his head, yawning, and sticking close to the shadows in the alleys behind the garden fences. He was missing a wedding ring.

In the garden behind Baker's Sweets, a woman knelt in the spring loam. Parting the soil, she took a gold wedding ring from her pocket and planted it as she would a seed. From a second-floor window, two curious eyes watched from behind the curtain, arms clutched tight around *A Tale of Two Cities.*

The woman in the garden stood, brushed her dirty hands on her skirt, and headed back inside.

On the village green, fat robins hopped to and fro looking for breakfast, ready to greet the new day. The last vestiges of dirty ice hiding in the shadows of cold alleys melted into dark stains on the pavement, drained down gutters, and trickled into the River Leam.

CHRISTMAS EVE, 1914
THE WESTERN FRONT

~ RODNEY STOKER ~

Exploding shells rattled my legs, my ribs, and my teeth. Reaching a hand to my ears, I felt warm blood. Warmth—warmth. I still had feeling left.

"Luther," I croaked, *"Luther."*

He was a motionless lump, rolled over on his belly, pressed right up against me. *Oh God. Was he—?*

I have no idea how long I laid there, the world flashing white and black with shell bursts, but I only managed to discern three thoughts from the jumble.

Appleby was standing right in front of the guns when the shell hit so there's no way he survived. If Appleby is dead, then the others probably are too. That means we are alone, and nobody is coming to rescue us.

Each thought took eons to take shape. I grappled for more, but everything slipped away in the fluctuating darkness and blinding white. I struggled to breathe. My voice was all but gone; pain came out in wheezes of spittle through gritted teeth. Each drop of rain or snow or falling debris burned.

"Our Father, who art in heaven, hallowed be thy name."
"Our Father, who art in heaven, hallowed be thy name."
"Our Father, who art in heaven, hallowed be thy name."

The rest of the prayer escaped me, and my brain prompted me to repeat the words on its own accord. Luther's face was hidden—his body dark and unmoving. And he had not written the letter to his mother.

"Forgive me, Constance Baker, full of grace; blessed art thou amongst women, and blessed is the fruit of thy womb."

The night flashed white with manufactured light as a flare rose into the sky like the Star of Bethlehem. A rising plume of dirt flew over us, and through some force of will I don't understand, I grabbed Luther's arm and dragged him with me as I rolled into the crater that had opened up behind me. The dirt settled back to the ground, half-burying us in our graves like a heavy blanket to block out the stinging air. To rest. I was a boy, cozy under blankets on Christmas Eve. I recalled Christmas Eve service, at midnight as Father Carmichael paced at the front of the church in his vestments. The church walls, the ribbed and cavernous belly of a whale, swallowed me up like the tales of old. The walls rose to the cloudy blanket in the pale hours of the coming day, crisscrossed with smoke trails from rockets and aeroplanes and mortars. I closed my eyes again, ready for a long, long rest.

Something moved and my eyes once again struggled open. Luther. He rolled over and sat up, cradling his head. He looked at his hands and his side, finding no wounds, and then caught sight of me. Barely breathing, I eyed him from beneath cracked lids.

"Rodney Stoker?" he mouthed. "You are hurt."

He leaned in closer. When I didn't react, he waved a hand in my face. Then, he kissed my forehead. With cupped hands, he removed the dirt from my still-breathing corpse, then stripped off his coat and laid it over me.

The white eye of noon hung in the now clear sky. Shells flashed in the distance. Every time a bomb sounded, Luther convulsed, pressed his hands against his ears and rocked back and forth. I watched him do that for hours as I slipped in and out of the dark. Finally, a lull in the fighting came. Luther struggled to his knees and then to his feet, poking his head out in the clear daylight, glancing over to where our boys sat in the pillboxes. Then he turned and looked back at the Germans. Back and forth he looked, his head ticking and tocking like a metronome. Then he decided to make a run for it, and started to scramble up the side of the crater.

"Stay," I wheezed, my voice like two scraping stones. I threw my arm out to grab Luther's ankle, the pain of movement slicing through me like a bayonet's blade.

"Wait for dark … they'll see." I knew his nerves were screaming at him to run for the trench, but he stopped and looked down at me. "Stay. Stay for your mum," I said. "Write that letter. In my pocket."

"I don't know my letters!"

"I know. I'm going to help, remember? Help me get the paper and pencil."

He slid down beside me and, gently, reached into my trouser pocket and pulled out the stationery and pencil.

"Help me sit up."

"You're hurt, Rodney Stoker."

"Nothing we can do about it right now."

With difficulty, he helped me to a sitting position, slipping the pencil and paper in my trembling hand.

"Pretend she's here. What do you want to tell her?"

"Tell her I'm scared, Rodney Stoker. Tell her I don't know where I am or what's happening to the world. Tell her the people don't want to kill each other, but they don't know how to stop. Why do they only love things that aren't real? Rules aren't real. Countries aren't real. People, people are real! Catch people when they fall! Hug people when they're sad! Laugh with people when they're happy! Is that so hard?"

I gritted my teeth as I tried bringing the pencil to the paper. For every word Luther said, I made sure to scribble something. My hand was trembling too much to write anything legible, but Luther didn't know that. So long as he kept talking, here, away from the crater's lip, I kept scribbling. A shell fell nearby, and the Earth shook, and he slammed his palms to his ears, shrieking and weeping and rocking, nose running, eyes red.

My voice was barely more than a raspy croak, but I tried to comfort him, to keep him from leaving our crater. "Keep talking. Think of your mum, now. Your mum."

He shouted fragments of words between infantile sobs, and I kept scribbling, pinning the stationery against my knee for a writing surface.

Another bomb, closer this time, knocked Luther on his back. He righted himself, plunged his hands into the mud, and pulled out two clumps. Tearing off chunks of it, his hands worked hard, spinning, rolling, flattening between his palms, churning out little marbles, little truffles that he laid in rows on the ground. Sobs punctuated his sentences, and he shouted staccato phrases that undulated in his throat and burst out his mouth like a sing-song lamentation.

"Tell her Rodney Stoker is afraid of me because I don't follow the rules. Tell her to stop following the rules that make her afraid. Tell her everyone is afraid of each other and they cry and point guns and think they are always right about everything. People who are big have big ideas that are too big to fit. Tell her everyone is afraid of themselves because they don't know who they are."

Luther wiped his nose.

"Tell her sometimes it's not so hard to stop being afraid; all you have to do is be smaller and quieter than scary things so they can't find you. Tell her it is good to live, to be happy and sad with people who work together and take care of each other, and they don't know it because they are not small and quiet enough and are always yelling the loudest because they think it makes them right, but they don't even hear their own words. Tell them all to be quiet inside and to listen so they don't have to be afraid."

For every bomb that fell that day, every cracking of the Earth itself, I flinched and waited for the end while Luther wept and rocked and made mud truffles. Appleby once told me that each time you're near an explosion, a little part of your brain rattles out of place and sort of drowns in fear. During heavy shelling, you have to keep your cool, or else your whole brain will drown in its own fear. He was right. I could feel the little parts of my brain screaming at me to run and hide, for to stay was certain death, but to run back to the trench was an even more certain death. And besides, I could no more run than I could be crowned king of the British Empire. Fear wrung me out. Adrenaline ran dry, and darkness seeped into the edge of my vision. My legs went stiff, and I dropped the pencil and couldn't bend my arms to pick it up. They paper fluttered away and the whole world was muted, a silent film, as Luther Baker and I waited for the end and everything spun and shattered around us.

~ JIM BAKER ~

I checked my watch. At this rate, I'd make it to Luther by the next morning. I slipped out the door and hopped off the train where my boots sank into an inch of mud. There was no shortage of mud in France; in fact the whole train yard was a frosted, churned-up mud pit. My fingers numbed in the freezer-burned air. I turned back and faced the train, not sure if I was supposed to hang back and help Private Roberts unload the post or not. *Eeh. It's his job, I'll just leave him to it.*

I pulled my boots out of the muck and suction-cupped my way across the muddy expanse, over to the cluster of buildings and the shed full of lorries. Guessed right—it was the post office. I told them my name and turned in my papers, and they held up their monocles to squint at them, and told me to come back at noon. Sure thing. Outside the post office and the warehouses and the depots, I found a dirt road that led into the nearby village of Hazebrouck. Maybe I could find a cafe there or something.

As I walked, I felt the ground rumble. I looked up, thinking a bomb was coming for me, but a few seconds passed, and nobody else panicked. I supposed it must be normal, this close to the fighting. On the horizon, I could see a grey smudge of smoke. That must be the front.

The town smelled of manure. It was a small cluster of homes and telegraph poles and shops rising out of a turnip field patchwork. Each home had a Christmas wreath on the door and smoke chugging out the chimney. I passed a group of children playing soccer with, of all people, a British soldier, and I wondered what would happen to the Moreau sisters. From the shop windows, a group of women looked on, arms crossed. An old lady was walking on the street near me, and I gave her a wide smile.

Around the corner, I chanced upon an open café with a nice courtyard where soldiers reclined at tables.

"Beer," I said, slapping a few coins down on the counter. I was apprehensive that the barkeeper would not understand English.

"Not enough. You want beer, you pay more." He held out his palm. "Only place for miles you can buy."

"Keep your beer, then," I shrugged. "Don't want to bargain with you. You got water?"

The bartender glared but poured me a short glass of water and slammed it down on the counter. I walked over to an empty table, listening as the other patrons talked about their days.

"The hospital is plenty busy; they've been shelling since last night."

"So much for Christmas cheer."

"Who's in your shift?"

"Mother Brand is leading it, which I guess is nice. She tends to keep people from losing their heads."

"That Ethyl sure is something, isn't she?"

What? I turned to see four men in dirty white coats—doctors, I presumed—smoking around a table. "Excuse me," I piped up, "did you say Ethyl Brand?"

One of them nodded, jetting out a ribbon of smoke and steam in the crisp air. "She works up in the hospital. Red Cross. Not here now, of course. She's gone down to the front to treat a poor bloke from the Royal Warwickshires. Hit by a shell."

"You called her Mother Brand, though," I said. "Is she a nun now?"

"Why, do you know her?"

"Grew up with her."

The doctor raised his eyebrows. "She's a mystery. Some days I think she's a nun, other days I think she's an atheist. Came here from Boulogne with the Carmelites. There's a convent a few miles out," he pointed. "They house whoever they have room for—nurses, beggars, and the like."

I nodded. Maybe I'd pay Ethyl a visit before I—well, it goes without saying.

I stared at the floor, and my breathing slowed. I was empty inside, resigned and unsure and terrified all at once. No matter. I'd made it this far and I had to keep focused on the goal. Instinctively I patted my bag where Luther's ticket to Algeria was stowed. After I made sure he was on his way, well, who knew what would happen after that. I rose from the table and stepped outside. My shadow stretched across the street in the red evening sky. Back to the post office I marched, my reserve wobbling.

"You alright?" a baby-faced officer called.

"Hmm," I nodded at him.

The lieutenant kept walking, and I paid him no mind until I heard him call out, "Hey, you! Girls! What are you doing?"

I turned and saw three little girls shrinking away from the officer's commanding voice. I stopped in my tracks. The girls from the train!

"Say, what are you doing here?" the officer approached them. "This is no place for little girls alone. Where are your parents?"

Celeste reached for her skirts, where I knew she kept her knife. She'd use it if he got too close, Of that, I had no doubt. But the consequences for pulling a weapon on an officer? They'd lock her away for sure. And then what would happen to the little ones?

"Excuse me, young lady," the lieutenant increased his pace, straggling after the three girls.

Pacing up behind the man, I grabbed him by the arm and. "Don't worry about these ragamuffins," I said. "I can take them to where they're supposed to be."

He looked me up and down with disdain. "How dare you grab me like that! Get your hand off me."

I let go and stepped back.

"Do you know these girls?" he asked.

"I am acquainted with them and know where they live. I'll see they get out of your way." Before he could protest, I ushered the girls down the street and around the corner.

When we were finally a few blocks away, I pushed them all into a little café and sat them down at a table in the darkest corner. Already, the whispers of *Pére Noël* sprang up.

"Let's quiet down about that, alright?" I said. "You want that officer sending the authorities after you? Sending you off to who knows where?"

Celeste looked at her two sisters and shook her head.

"Right. So it looks like you'll need to lay low for a few hours. Are you hungry?"

Hungry appeared to be a word all three girls knew for they all three leaned forward as if I'd already laid out a buffet dinner.

"Okay," I said. "I'll buy you some food."

I asked the bartender what food they had, and he just said, "Soup." I fished out a few coins and carried back a small loaf of bread and three bowls of pink broth swimming with boiled beets. It was more water than soup, but the girls slurped it down in no time at all. I took the empty bowls up and paid for a refill.

"Where did you come from?" I asked Celeste. "Where are your parents?"

"We come from Lorraine," Celeste began. "Soldiers come in the fall. They say they not hurt us, but when it was cold and we looked forward to Christmas, then our town burned down, and we knew the truth. I think they must hate Christmas. *Ils dètestent noël.*"

She rattled off a few sentences in French, like she was translating our conversation for her sisters, then continued.

"After the fire, we left. There were many of us at first, and we walked through farms and villages. People called us *règièes*. One farmer gave us shoes when ours wore out. When it got too cold, a man gave us blankets." She gestured wrapping a blanket about herself. "Nuns took some of us away, but not all. We told them we had *un oncle*, old man, who lives in the North. It's our only family. So they put us on train and we go across France to find him. We come long way. But now it is Christmas, and you find us. You give us presents. You are our *Pére Noël*. You will take us to uncle at North Pole."

She nodded to her sisters, and they looked up at me with wide eyes as if I was St. Nick himself. Jesus, Mary, and Joseph, I about wept.

It wasn't so much the suffering that struck me—I had seen suffering before. But these little girls didn't even know the meaning of war. They'd been so traumatized they'd gone searching for a folk tale. Santa Claus, for God's sake! Santa Claus would give them presents. Santa Claus would take care of them. Santa Claus would take them to their uncle, the only family they had left. Jesus. To hell with Europe. To hell with this war. All this death and destruction for the whims of a handful of incestuous Kings, Kaisers, Czars, whatever damn titles they could make up for themselves. Cowards all. None of them were on the front lines, putting their own bodies in danger. Every damn one of them would probably flee if the enemy was at their gates, burning down their towns.

"You want me to take you to the North Pole? To find your uncle?" I repeated, swallowing hard.

Celeste nodded.

"You sure your uncle lives there?"

Another nod.

"Does your North Pole happen to be in the French countryside?" I asked.

"*Oui monsieur.*"

Celeste shoved a letter toward me. The French was indecipherable to me, but she pointed out the address.

Albert Moreau

Estaires, France

"Is this your uncle? Albert Moreau? Living in Estaires?" Celeste nodded.

I checked my watch, pulled out my map, and found Estaires. Damn. That's not too far from where I was headed. I'd have time to get them to their uncle and still get to Luther by morning. Bloody hell. Looked like I was going to be St. Nick for the night.

"Okay girls, it looks like we're making a stop at the North Pole."

The Moreau sisters looked at each other and then swarmed around me, hugging me around the waist and hanging on me as if I were their long-lost uncle.

Or *Pére Noël.*

JUNE, 1848

LEAMINGTON SPA, ENGLAND

~ JIM BAKER ~

"After I had Rodney down, I took his blasted knife and threw it right into the water there." I pointed to the middle of the river.

"What set him off this time?" Ethyl asked. She was leaning against an old log with her knitting, working the wool over the needles while I waded barefoot at the water's edge.

"Sometimes, I think he knocked something loose in his head when Luther pushed him down. We used to play fight all the time, but not anymore. Rodney is always paranoid now. Jumpy. Always looking behind his back and getting angry whenever someone makes a funny joke about him. He's always liked weapons, but then he started carrying that blasted knife with him all the time and pulling it out whenever anyone, including me, got too close, which kind of scared me. He never cut me, until today." I touched my arm where Rodney's knife had drawn blood. "He was afraid to before. I mean we we've been best friends forever, and I guess he was always afraid Luther would appear and knock him down again. But Luther wasn't around and maybe he wasn't so scared."

Ethyl frowned and her needles clicked a bit faster. "Does you arm hurt?"

"No. It's just a scratch."

"I don't like this, Jim. Rodney's tough talk … it's like he has to prove something. And now, he's gone and actually attacked you."

"I don't think he meant to hurt me. He was as shocked as I was. Still, I'm glad I threw that knife away." I looked out at the center of the Leam and wondered where the knife would end up. Would it float to the sea or sink into the sediment and stay there till some bloke found it a thousand years from now? "Rodney says he's going to join the army, you know. Plans to go serve in India or something. He won't join the navy; says they don't get enough action. And he never stops talking about guns. One time after school, he went on forever about what kind of gun he would use if England was ever attacked. He was hardly even paying attention to me, and I don't think he noticed when I got up to go see if Mum had any deliveries I needed to take care of."

"If he was willing to hurt you, he could hurt anyone," Ethyl said. "He just seems on edge all the time now."

"Nah, he's not really violent. Just .. touchy. But you're right on one account. I don't think there's a group Rodney doesn't have a problem with. Irish, Germans, French. Even his mum. He says he hates his mum because she's too protective and treats him like a baby, and he doesn't say too much good about most anyone else. He never questions

Father Carmichael or his own father, though. He never questions anyone in charge, just those he thinks hurt his pride. And he never questions the old veterans who drink at the pub smoking cigars and drinking and swearing that *kids these days are too damn soft.*" I looked over at her. "He doesn't say anything bad about you, though." I waited for a reaction, but Ethyl didn't look up.

"Why are you even still friends with him? If he's treats everyone so poorly—especially Luther—just cut off contact with him." She was knitting so fast that she kept dropping a stitch and having to go back.

"I don't know. Old habits, maybe. Or remembering good times. Maybe I feel guilty about Luther pushing him. Usually whenever Rodney gets going on about guns or war or killing people, I just laugh and say with his luck, Luther would probably be sent to the front with him. Whenever I mention Luther, Rod flinches and touches his head. Before I thought Rodney understood about Luther, but after … well, now he's just like everyone else. They all think Luther is some kind of scary monster for being a little different."

"People are afraid of what they don't understand, and they don't understand Luther" Ethyl said. "I know you want to defend him, but you can't lose control and be angry all the time over it. My aunt's a nun you know, and she says, 'The closer to self-control, the closer to power.' She's very smart. Maybe you could take a page from her."

"That's what I don't like about people, large groups of people—they're afraid of everything. And when people are afraid, they get to acting tough and talking big—history and politics and whatnot. They get to being like Rod and lashing out to try and convince themselves they're not afraid. But damnit, I swear I'll hit back every time. Just like when I was little, and I'd take on the bullies Luther's age when they made fun of him. I may have stumbled home bruised and without shoes, but at least I stood up for my brother. Someone—including Rod—hits me and mine, I will always hit back."

"*God's sake, Jim.*" Ethyl put down her knitting and scowled up at me. "You're as bad as Rodney!"

"It's the ones who don't care one way or another that live best. I don't care that Luther is different. In fact, I don't care about him at all. Or Mum. Or the Stokers or Father Carmichael or anyone."

"You are ridiculous. Of course you care. If you didn't, you wouldn't strike back."

"You're wrong, Ethyl, I don't care. It's just that you can't let people take advantage and run right over you."

"You care about your aunt Lavinia. And I thought we were friends. I thought you cared about me.

"Well—" I started, but Ethyl kept going.

"You care, but you refuse to admit it because you think it makes you weak. You don't understand that weakness is denying your honest and true feelings because of what someone else might think. You already lost to Rodney when you surrendered your peace of mind to him. That's what the nuns would say."

I didn't want to think she was right, so I ignored what she said and looked at the river. I would have to be home soon, anyway. Today was Luther's birthday, and we were throwing him a party at dinnertime. Besides, I had other things to think about.

"There's something else I have to tell you," I mumbled. "I found some pamphlets at my house the other day, for a boarding school. I think Mum is sending me off."

"That's great news," Ethyl said. She sounded enthusiastic, but she didn't look it.

I frowned at her.

"You're very lucky to be going somewhere you can get a good quality education."

"You don't understand."

"Understand what?" Ethyl said.

"Mum's doing this to get back at me. She's out to get me, you see."

"And you said Rodney was paranoid. I can't listen to this any longer, Jim." She stood and started packing up her yarn and needles.

"Won't you be sad?"

"At what?"

"When I leave for boarding school?"

Ethyl looked at me straight in the face. "I'm going to become a nun, Jim."

"*What?*"

"I've been telling you about the missions in Africa for weeks. I'm actually very excited. It means a lot to me that I might be able to help people who need so much."

II felt the color in my cheeks and I shook my head.

"Do you care truly about me, then?" Ethyl asked. "I care about you, too, but I'm decided. I want to do something important with my life. I want something more."

Behind me, the river twirled and sparkled as it flowed toward the sea. In the green shadows beneath the stuffy trees, I looked at her eyes and her red hair that turned gold on the edges where strands floated like spider silk.

"Remember when I tried to dance with you at your Aunt Lavinia's wedding? It was a long time ago, I know, but—"

"Yes."

"You pulled your hands away and ran because you were embarrassed."

"I remember." I looked away.

"When you pulled my hair? Did you do that to act tough? Were you afraid like Rodney?"

"I—I—I guess." I exhaled heavily and shrugged, picking at a low-hanging leaf

"What were you afraid of?" She said it casually, like she didn't know the answer, like she was talking about philosophy or something.

"I don't know what you're talking about, and I'd appreciate it if you stopped nosing around in my business." I hated myself as soon as I said it. I picked up my shoes, stepped past her, and climbed over the old stone wall.

"Where are you going?"

"It's Luther's birthday. I'm going to eat some cake."

"Running away again." The words stung, but I didn't look back as I crossed the uphill slope from the river, where the sheep grazed without noticing me. At the other end of the pasture, I jumped over the other wall, stopped to put on my shoes, and then headed down the sunbaked path until I got back into town.

I walked in the back door and headed for the dining room where Luther, Mum, Aunt Lavinia, and Uncle Mark were already sitting.

"What happened to your arm?" Mum snapped.

Dammit! I rolled my sleeves down and looked away. Too late. Mum had her fingers around my wrist. She stood and dragged me into the kitchen.

"Who was it this time? Rodney again?"

"He was carrying that knife of his and salivating over guns and stuff. And besides, he started it. I was doing everyone a favor."

"Listen, *Jim,*" she said my name whenever she was serious, but this was the first time she'd ever said it with contempt, like she said Margie Stoker's name. "You know Rodney knows Luther's the one what pushed him. The only reason he doesn't blab it all over town is because he's embarrassed. You piss him off enough, and he won't care—he'll tell. You want that to happen? You want your brother to end up institutionalized?"

"What do you want me to do? Rodney starts fights with everyone these days. Should I let him beat me up?"

"You're the only one in this house who can prevent Rodney from hurting Luther."

"Why does Luther have to be the center of everything? All I want is a big brother like the other boys have—he'd teach me to fight and help me cheat at tests and show me how to get girls to like me. If I want to have fun with Luther, I have to explain things to him twenty times and he still won't get it. And he doesn't like me, either. Every time I touch him, he goes off!"

I'd rehearsed that speech every night for what seemed like years. It felt good to finally say it, but now that it was out, I was afraid something inside me would break, that I would start crying because I knew the truth. That Luther was the center of everything and that everything in our family was about Luther. About saving Luther, protecting Luther, keeping Luther out of trouble and out of a sanitarium. To the extent that Mum cared about me, it was just so I could some day take care of Luther when she was gone. Ethyl Brand was right about me. I was afraid. Afraid I would never have a life of my own. Never have someone who loved me for me, instead of for what I could do for Luther.

Through the dining room door, I could hear Luther stringing sentences together about cake and presents. He was talking better these days, but he didn't like all the attention of being the birthday boy. When Aunt Lavinia began tapping on the table to recall his attention, he started flapping his hands. Aunt Lavinia had known Luther his whole life and Uncle Mark had been around for years, but only Mum and I knew Luther well enough to read the subtle signs. We had that much in common, and the same alarms went off in our brains, giving us the same terrors, the same annoyances, the same hopes.

Mum exhaled, gave me a nod, and headed back toward the dining room. On the way out of the kitchen, I glanced at the work table where there was an unfinished batch of truffles. There must've been a hundred of the coin-sized jewels, with a bowl of rich ganache next to a plate of nuts. I loved the days when Mum made truffles. I would sometimes help, but I would always watch and smell. I knew the motions well—cut the chocolate, melt it down, add the cream, stir the ganache, and roll the truffles into marbles between cocoa-powdered palms. Beside the bowl, I noticed another boarding school pamphlet.

"Is it true?" I waved the pamphlet at her. "Are you sending me away?"

"Listen, I need you to work with me, Jim. We don't have a normal family. People don't know what to make of us and so they talk. You need to get away from here because you're not going to make it if you turn sour. People on top, they can get as sour as they want because everyone cares what they think. We are the people on the bottom, and we have to keep our heads down, smile, say yes sir and yes ma'am to everyone who asks. You need to learn how to do that, Jim, or you won't make it in the world."

"Think I don't know that?" I swallowed hard and blinked at her.

"You're the only one in this family who has a chance of rising up above"—she swept an arm around the room—"above all this. If you do well at school, you'll get a job and enough money to take care of Luther after I'm gone."

"No." I shook my head. "I don't want to go. You can't make me."

"Yes, I can," she said and went back into the dining room.

I followed, of course. Aunt Lavinia looked up when I walked back in and then looked over at Luther who was now rocking back and forth in his chair, making bubbles on his tongue and staring at the cake. He grabbed for the cake and Aunt Lavinia caught his hand and pulled it back. I was so mad I grabbed his gift—Dad's copy of *A Tale of Two Cities*—and slammed it down on his plate, cracking it.

"Happy Birthday, Luther."

He squealed and slapped my arm.

"Jim, now, no need to upset him." Aunt Lavinia took on that high-pitched, ragged edge.

"Doesn't matter. You'll all be rid of me soon enough."

Aunt Lavinia's eyes widened, and Luther smashed his fist into the cake, squelching the iced *Happy 10th Birthday!* into a ball of frosting that squeezed through his fingers and into the wrinkles of his knuckles and the cracks of his fingernails. He made that moaning sound that sounded almost inhuman and then jumped up on his chair.

Uncle Mark looked petrified. He glanced at Aunt Lavinia for assurance that everything was perfectly normal, and she shrugged and tried not to make a big deal of it.

"Luther, sit down." Mum tried to sound nice in front of Mark. I knew she didn't want them—her own family—to see a full-blown episode with the hitting, the pillows, the grappling and pinning down on the rug. Same old, same old. Just not in front of the guests.

But Luther was too far gone. He ran out of the dining room, into the kitchen, and in circles around the house like he always does before he bursts. Any second and he'd stop to bash himself against the wall and start hitting himself.

Mum gave me the death glare, and then turned to go fetch him.

"Luther, Luther," she kept calling with that high-pitched voice, trying to sound nice.

What was she hoping for? Anyone could tell Luther had passed the point of no return; his meltdown would keep boiling until he reached his final form—fetal position, holding his head, tucked away in a corner, not responding to sound or touch. But Mum was trying to pretend things were dandy, and Aunt Lavinia was going along with it. She directed Uncle Mark's attention to the nice clock that Granny left us.

Meanwhile, Luther ran into the kitchen, pulling his hair and moaning. I stepped into the doorway. He looked like he was in so much pain. He didn't like loud noises, I knew that, so why did I have to slam the book in front of him? I just needed to control myself. Mum knew it, I knew it, but that didn't change anything right now. I'd tipped Luther over the edge. It was my fault his birthday was ruined.

Mum ran after Luther, opening her arms to lock him in a hug that would prevent him from hitting himself, but she couldn't catch him. Luther and Mum found themselves facing each other on opposite ends of the big truffle-dotted island in the middle of the kitchen.

He looked up at Mum and then at the truffles. Mum, truffles. Mum, truffles.

In the dining room, Aunt Lavinia and Uncle Mark spoke in hushed tones.

"Luther, please," Mum whispered, "don't do it. Control yourself, just this once. We wouldn't want to cause a ruckus for Uncle Mark now, would we?"

Mum bowed her head down on the island, covering her face with her own hair. She was begging him, and yet, Luther probably didn't even hear her. Mum knew that, right? She had to.

Luther looked at her, then at the truffles again. He picked one up and held it close to his eye, studying every facet down to the fingerprints and palm lines left over from the rolling. He held it to his nose and inhaled. His eyebrows knit and forehead wrinkled, and then he reached into the big copper bowl of ganache and pulled out a clump the size of his fist. Tearing it into ten chunks, he took each between his flattened palms and rolled them into little balls.

When the shrieks and hitting never came, Mum looked up. She gasped and put a hand over her mouth.

"Oh my..." I turned to see Aunt Lavinia peeking into the kitchen, touching her cross necklace. Uncle Mark stood behind her, asking what was going on in a whisper.

Luther ignored them all, rolling out truffles between his palms. His whole universe had narrowed down to those truffles and everything else must have faded to him. The first one took about ten seconds, but he kept got faster and faster. Soon, he had the entire surface of the table covered in truffles. Occasionally, he'd pat his hands with flour, just like he'd watched Mum do his whole life, just as deftly, just as naturally, just as rhythmically as a concert pianist, a genius at peace. It's like he was back in Mum's womb, safe and quiet. His chest rose, rose, rose, rose, rose, and then fell, fell, fell, fell, fell. And he kept making truffles. By the time the copper bowl was empty, his eyebrows flattened, his licked his lips as if he were parched, and then calmly walked over to the cupboard and climbed inside. He pulled the door shut, and it clicked behind him.

◆●◆

When my eyes cracked open, the first thing I noticed was the battering wind outside and the walls of the house creaking. A storm must have blown in because it was still dark and the rain didn't just patter on the roof but pounded sideways against the walls and window panes. Was it even morning? What if it was only midnight and the storm had woken me up?

Oh well. I knew I'd have plenty of time to sleep on the train to Rugby the next day. That's where I was headed, to the boarding school in Rugby, the same town Mum was born in. She said she knew the headmaster when they were both kids and that he was being especially kind letting me in and *blah blah blah*. Apparently, Ethyl was right. It would be a chance for a good education as Mum kept stressing that the classes were a lot better than the classes at the country school in Leamington.

Other boys from Leamington were headed to the school in Rugby, too, Rodney among them. He said there'd be hundreds of boys, all crammed together in one house without any privacy. All my life, I'd seen the boarding school boys during Christmas and summer breaks when they'd come home on holiday. They would wear their suits and ties and hang around the country school house, leaning on walls and throwing cricket balls and squeak-laughing and hitting each other. They'd swear loudly and curse their mothers' graves whenever they stubbed their toes. In fact, they swore loudly about pretty much everything, but only when they were the oldest ones around. Their faces were red and agitated with pimples and scars, and they had little fuzzy beards and little fuzzy mustaches they weren't sure if they should shave yet. Their favorite topic of discussion was the penis, something I still hadn't quite come to terms with.

I already knew how school would turn out. First day, some older boys would gang up on me in the loo or something. They'd steal all my clothes while I slept or bathed. It happened to everyone. But I'd get through It.

Luther wouldn't be there.

And only the Leamington boys would even know who Luther was and none of them would care, besides Rodney. In fact, there would be nobody to make fun of Luther. And with no one to make fun of Luther, there would be no one for me to fight. This could be really great, actually. But I couldn't let Mum know that. I had to keep pretending to be angry or she'd figure it out.

I rolled out of bed and put some clothes on. The wind kept battering against the walls, and I felt a draft that made me shiver and want to crawl back under the covers. I pulled my undershirt over my head, buttoned my shirt, belted my trousers, and tried to figure out how to tie the tie. It was a red and gold and matched the colors of the school. Finally, I just left it hanging around my neck and put on the jacket. There, I looked fit and proper like one of the squeak-laughing boys with the pimples. Oh joy—I was a wonder to behold.

I purposely left my bed sheets crooked and untidy and grabbed my luggage cases. I looked around my room before I left. Of course, it was empty now, everything packed away in my cases, but I felt like I was supposed to look it over and say good-bye. Only, it was four rickety wood walls that didn't give a damn one way or the other. So, I shrugged and shut the door.

In the stairway, I passed all the awards Luther had won over the summer.

The Great Warwickshire Baking Contest
Third Place

The Great Leamington Bake-Off
Second Place

The Great Candy Exhibit, London
Best Chocolate Artisan

There were photographs of Luther standing open-mouthed next to famous chefs whose names I couldn't even pronounce. There was a blue ribbon from the Warwick County Fair and a newspaper clipping that read *BAKER'S TRUFFLES ARE NO TRIFLE.* I remembered going to these contests and watching the other red-faced chefs. They would throw their towels down and yell, then run a hand through their hair to cool down. And Luther would step up to the table, just like he always did, face empty, eyes only for his bowl of ganache. He would pat his hands in flour and roll those truffles better than anyone in the whole of England.

Girls would giggle when he looked at them, and he would show his teeth.

What surprised me the most were his sentences. When girls came up to him, he would say things like "I make candy. I watch Mum. You want my candy." He would try and put candy in their mouths, and they loved it. It turned out that baking shows were the only places where social boundaries didn't matter.

When I made it down to the kitchen the next morning, Luther was already there, rolling out a hundred truffles just to get the day started. The thing was, we knew he'd sell most of them that day, too. More people started coming to the shop once they heard rumors about Luther the Truffler. Mum even cleaned the place up, and we all painted the walls pink, and polished the shelves until they shined with the chocolate coins and sugared jewels under glass. The place was really coming back to life, like it had been before Luther arrived and Dad died. Occasionally, Luther would speak with people, too. He was getting better every day, but sometimes he'd be really quiet and nervous. Still he put words and sentences together, and, strangely enough, people were charmed by him. He had turned into a good looking bloke and when he wasn't flapping his hands, hitting himself in the head, or running around like a madman, he seemed almost normal. At least when he was in the kitchen. Which was where he was now. I stopped in the doorway and said good morning. He glanced up from his work.

"Why do you have bags?"

"I'm going to the boarding school this year, remember?"

No answer. He returned to his work, and I smiled.

"You know, you should give some of those truffles to Ethyl one of these days."

"Why?"

"She—she'd like it. She's nice. A lot of the girls in town made fun of you before, but Ethyl never did.

"I know."

"But now that you're famous, even the ones who made fun of you talk about you and think you're cute."

"I am cute."

I laughed. I found myself walking over to the mantle, where all of Dad's books still sat next to our grandfather clock. Funny they called it that, when really it belonged to my grandmother. I still had a few of those books to read, including Byron's poems. I personally hated Byron, but I had to do it to know what Dad was like. I had to. And if Dad was a hopeless romantic, then so be it. In a way, those books were my Dad, still alive with all his opinions and morals. They had done more to raise me than any teacher or priest or old man or mother I knew. Except maybe Aunt Lavinia.

I stood there, staring at the books for a while, when I heard Mum's steps coming down the stairs, fully dressed and ready for the day. First thing she did was give Luther a kiss on the forehead.

"Jim," she called from the kitchen, "it's eight o'clock. We were supposed to leave fifteen minutes ago. Get your bags to the door."

She had just appeared, and I was staring right at the clock and it said 7:45. She wanted to play this game now? On the day I was leaving? God damn. I took that book of Byron and shoved it in my suitcase, just to show her.

I met Mum by the door. She called for Luther to hurry, and the two of us stepped onto the street. When Luther emerged, Mum locked the door behind us. At least, the rain had stopped. Still the cobblestones shone in the grey light. When I thought about it, they were only dry maybe ten, twenty days a year at most. We walked a short way down Bath Street and under the train bridge where all the rats and rubbish usually settled, passing Doc Abbott's on the way. Down High Street a little way, there was the train station. I couldn't figure why my stomach was churning, so I decided I was angry. At Mum? Of course at Mum.

"One to Rugby, thank you." Mum slipped a fold of money under the glass window, then handed me my ticket.

I tucked it in my trousers before I could get a good look at it. I didn't want to see it.

And who else did we see waiting at the station but Mr. Stoker himself.

"Jim, good man." He walked up to shake my hand, stiff and gruff, in a full suit. "Now, I like to see this. I know you and Rodney have had a falling out of late, but I like to see that you're going to a proper school, nonetheless. Nothing like a good English education to turn boys into men."

I shook his hand, and his grip was tight. He didn't let go of my hand but instead bent down to inspect it.

"Fiiiine grip, lad, a trigger grip if I ever saw one. You'll make a fine soldier one day, my boy. Just like Rodney. You'll be a service to king and country, I'm certain of it." He turned to Luther and looked him up and down and then turned back to me. "I suppose the burden of serving your family and your nation must fall to you, considering your brother's state—"

"I see you bought a new wedding ring?" Mum interrupted, nodding at his fat fingers.

"Uh, what? Excuse me. I must rejoin Mrs. Stoker. Good day to you, Mrs. Baker. Jim." Mr. Stoker wet his lips, tipped his hat at us, and walked back over to where Rodney and Mrs. Stoker sat on the bench, awaiting the train to Rugby as well.

Mrs. Stoker and Rodney watched the exchange but said nothing.

And that's how I left home to become a man. Watching the train station roll by in a car crammed full of eight-year-olds, and my older brother talking for the first time in complete sentences, as if the prospect of me leaving had set him free.

CHRISTMAS EVE, 1914

THE WESTERN FRONT

~ LUTHER BAKER ~

Rodney Stoker told me to follow him onto the field and to leave the trench and we crawled in lots of mud and then the sky rained bombs and then he pushed me in the big hole and said hide and wrote a letter to Mum for me. Rodney Stoker said do not go outside the crater do not leave until they come for you and it was light and the guns would see do not step outside. But we had to get back to pals where there were no bombs and there was food. I was very afraid and the sounds went away and the feelings went away and there were truffles. Truffles in my hands that I made best. Little candies to give to happy kids that giggle and girls that giggle and say they like me and I blush like at the candy contest. *Happy happy happy happy not here not here not here not here*. Why isn't everyone happy? Why do they want to hurt each other? Why? Why? Why? Why do they shoot at me and scare me so bad my thoughts stop and I stop. Why do they throw bombs that shriek so loud they made me feel like my head is broken? But Rodney Stoker really was broken.

Blood turned brown and crusty in places blood wasn't supposed to be like when I pushed him down when he was little. His skin was red and hot and his hair was gone and he was bald. Rodney Stoker's arms turned into wood because they would not bend and he didn't answer any of my questions and didn't talk or look at my eyes. I was dead for the whole day. The bombs stopped when it was dark and I turned alive again and my thoughts started thinking again. I thought they would come back but they didn't. I wanted to look over the edge but everyone who did it died. And Rodney Stoker told me not to so I didn't know what to do. I asked Rodney Stoker can I look over the edge to go back to get a doctor but he didn't answer and I tried to poke him and lift him but his legs were stiff like wood just like his arms. So I sat there until it was darker and my thoughts came back because the bombs weren't making them go away. If I didn't look over the edge we would not be able to go be safe and we would stay here and I did not want to stay here. So I looked over the edge and there was nothing. The world was flat and grey even though there used to be trees. The guns did not make noise but I didn't know if they saw me so I hid again in the big hole. I didn't know what to do if I should stay or leave we would get killed. *What do I do, Mum?* I cried a little and crawled around the big hole. I saw the letter Rodney Stoker wrote and stuffed it in my pocket because I had to send it to Mum so she would not be sad and know I was okay. I had to get out and send the letter to Mum. I had to get out and send the letter to Mum. A man was standing on top and looking at me with a gun he was a German because he had a pointy hat and a mustache. But he talked normal and said hello are you stuck. He talked English like me. We looked at each other and I was not scared because he was a person and people I knew usually tried to help other people so I said yes I need help am I allowed to leave the hole my friend is hurt bad. He said yes but not now. He said wait. He said words I did not know and looked around and told me to be quiet and stay still and he would be back when it was safe. So I waited because I did not want to die and I did not want Rodney Stoker to die. I thought maybe he would not come back and then he did. He told me the bombs were going to stop for a while and I could take my friend for help if he was still alive. I had been checking and Rodney Stoker was still alive, but almost not. Then the German crawled into the hole with me and crouched down beside Rodney Stoker. He looked at me and said it is Christmas and he and his friends do not want to fight now and if he lets me go can I tell my friends that the Germans will not shoot if the Brits do not shoot. I said I do not want to fight anymore at all especially at Christmas and so I would tell my friends. And he gave me a note with some words on it and I put it in my pocket with my letter to Mum. Then he helped me pick up Rodney Stoker because Rodney Stoker did not get up and he was heavy to carry but I was big. And he helped me get Rodney Stoker out of the hole and I said thank you. And the German shook my hand and told me Merry Christmas and please don't shoot on Christmas day and maybe even a week or so after that and did I have his note?

"Yes, I have the note in my pocket but I cannot read the words so I will give it to one of my friends."

"No officers," he said. "Don't show it to an officer or everything will be ruined."

"Okay," I said. I told him I liked the idea of no shooting. Especially at Christmas time. No one should be shooting anyone. Everyone should be eating candy.

~ JIM BAKER ~

We rode for the North Pole. The lorry bounced over the crest of the hill at top speed, the pedal touching the floor. I kept checking the sun as it set out the window, hoping this side trip wouldn't take too long.

"Any preferences?" The post master had asked.

"Ploegsteert," I'd answered as he threw me the keys to a beat up lorry. Postal workers started heaving the sacks in place, and after I was all loaded, I drove a few miles out of Hazebrouck, where I stopped to pick up Celeste, Adele, and Bernadette at an old windmill, our designated meeting point. Somehow, they managed to squeeze into the passenger seat. That was just as well, because I would've had to clear a space amid the cargo for them.

"All settled?" I tried sounding cheerful, but it was fake. I'd seen many adults put on that face when things threatened to spiral out of control, like Auntie Lavinia. I decided that wasn't for me.

Auntie Lavinia. My throat, constricted, as if stuck on a stone that wouldn't budge up or down.

I drove north, directly away from Ploegsteert, blazing down the dirt roads, over crests, and around curves. Every so often, we'd come across a crater, and I'd have to slow down and go around it. The grey folds of farmland sprawled out under the bruised sky—the blotchy lavenders skirting the clouds, the sun now gone away for her long nap.

I returned my gaze to the road, flipping the headlights on. The girls smiled at the sunset and made occasional comments to each other as we passed cows and sheep grazing peacefully as if there was not a war going on just a few miles away.

"Do you know how to get to your uncle's house," I asked Celeste.

"We haven't been there in a long time." Her voice was small and worried.

"Well," I said, trying to sound confident, "we'll find it together."

Every once in a while, we'd slow down at a crossroads to shine the headlights on a wooden sign with arrows pointing to the names of villages carved on them. With the map I'd been given, I followed the signs from town to town, clunking along lonely roads and through sleepy village squares. Soon the girls had bowed their heads together in the seat, eyes closed, breathing softly. At one stop, I threw my blanket over them. When my eyelids felt heavy and my head swayed, I sat up straighter and gripped the steering wheel harder. *Couple more miles to go.* I checked my watch—10:39 PM. *Damn.* How far was I from Ploegsteert?

Then I saw it. *Estaires,* the sign said in the headlights.

Yes.

It was now completely dark, and I cruised in to the village, trying to guess where the uncle's house would be. We passed the local church, glowing from within, and I could hear people caroling *in excelsis deo* as it echoed off of the brick and out Into the night. It was a warm, liquid sound that filled me up and I swallowed hard and tried not to think of Mum alone on Christmas Eve worrying about Luther. I checked my watch. One hour to midnight.

An old man walked down the side of the road, and I stopped beside him. "*Maison Albert Moreau?*" I said. The old man peered into the car at me. He was bundled in a heavy coat, and his face was hidden. He shook his head, mumbled something in a guttural French I couldn't understand, and pointed down the road and out toward the countryside. "How far? Kilometers?" I asked. The old man held up two fingers and then started in with the incomprehensible French again, so I told him thank you and drove off. I figured if I couldn't find the uncle's house first, I'd turn around and we could go into the church and ask someone after the service.

I started down the road the old man indicated. Two kilometers. So a little over a mile. Not far at all. As I drove out of town, I got the feeling that the war had skipped over this village. Hadn't seen a single soldier or crater anywhere. It seemed peaceful, and I felt good about leaving the girls with their uncle—if I could actually find him.

The road was little more than two worn tire tracks straddling a strip of prickly grass, so I had to go slow. It had seen more donkeys than autocars, I'd wager. On each side, the wood fences ran on without end. *Where's the cottage?*

Finally, in the distance. I saw the dark outline of a cottage and barn and turned down a lane that looked like it hadn't seen traffic since the Romans. I pulled up in front of the dark house, and the girls, hearing the engine shut off and the car stop moving, slowly raised their heads. I stepped outside. The grass crunched under my feet, frozen under a glittering frost. But still, no snow. Checked my watch again—11:20.

"Here?" Celeste tugged my sleeve.

There was no movement and no light. Maybe the uncle was at church after all. Beyond fifty meters, the world faded to dark outlines and hulking shapes. To the left was a row of trees, while to the right I assumed was another field. Above, the stars were striking—wide streaks of silver and gold, nebulae still blooming in the firmament. It was silent and sparkling, tender in its vastness.

I opened the back and pulled my torch out of my pack. "This way," I motioned to Celeste, who in turn motioned to her sisters.

My boots crunched on the frozen dirt, and I heard their light feet crunching after me. I shone the light over the cottage as we approached and then stopped. At its heart, the cottage was missing a whole bite out of its roof—shattered with boards sticking out like broken bones. I walked around the side and saw that all the windows had been blown out, walls were missing, and the furnishings were charred splinters. No one had been living there for a while.

I had been wrong earlier—the war had touched every town, every family. Including the Moreau's.

Bernadette threw her traitorous dolls at the ground when she saw it. She was cranky, cold, and hungry and up way past her bedtime, without a bed or anyone to tuck her in. Her nose ran, and hot tears fell down her cheeks. It was so cold that I could see fog coming off of her wet, red eyes. Tears are always lonely, so soon, Adele was sniffling as well. Celeste pulled them both close to her, assuring them that Peré Noël would not pass them by this year because they could not find a mantle to set their shoes on.

My watch now said a quarter to midnight. Was there an inn where I could drop them off? It was too late for that; the inns were all closed. There was the church we'd passed back in town. Midnight Mass would just be ending.

I pulled the girls in close—the tallest barely reached up to my chest—and hugged them tight. "Come on. Let's go back to the church in town."

AUGUST, 1914
LEAMINGTON SPA, ENGLAND

~ THE VILLAGE ~

In the morning, the newspaper boy gripped his bicycle handles and pedaled over to the *Leamington Courier*, a squat, square building that smelled of grease and ink. Next to the rush of the mechanical printers, the publisher, with his first three buttons open and sweat stains darkening his shirt, handed over the daily papers. His frown was deeper than usual. Every day, even in the heat, the newspaperman puffed on his daily cigar and pulled from the half empty bottle of Scotch on his desk. He needed the Scotch, he'd say, after reading the day's headline. After today's headline, he'd likely finish the bottle.

The newspaper boy handled the stack, tied with brown string, and dropped them in his basket. When he caught a glimpse of the headline, his dreams of running the *Leamington Courier* ended forever. He didn't know it then, but he would never fall in love, never get married, never become a father. He would never get to tell his children about that moment, the moment he became a man—or at least wanted to become one.

He pedaled down the street faster even than the cars, throwing papers toward marked doorposts as he went. As the news made its way through the village and surrounding countryside, mothers clung to first-born sons eager to prove themselves, fathers dug out old letters from their brothers, and uncles who died in the Boer War. Flags snaked up their poles; trumpets drowned out the singing of birds; churches assembled—some praying for peace and others for glorious victory. Father Carmichael, while sipping his coffee, read the morning paper and wrote a letter to his brother, wishing him best of luck and a safe return. In the envelope, he enclosed a rosary.

Mrs. Lavinia Bell went without breakfast that day and met her husband where he was sorting mail at the post office. In hushed tones, they discussed their future, during which Lavinia threw the paper in his face and stormed out in tears.

On the way home, she stopped by Baker's Sweets, where the newspaper still lay on the doorstep below a sign that read *Closed, Away at Baking Competition*. Lavinia unlocked the door, walked through the shop, and put the paper on the kitchen table, where a week's worth of mail waited for her sister's return.

Across town, Mrs. Margie Stoker prepared a hearty English breakfast for her husband. Out of habit, he frowned at his empty plate and rolled his replacement wedding ring. From the kitchen, Margie brought out a plate of toast, tomatoes, blood sausage, and bacon. While he started in on breakfast, Margie went to the door and fetched the daily paper and post in her robe. As she went back inside, she sorted through the stack of letters to find a note from Rodney, now stationed at Shorncliffe Barracks with the Royal Warwickshires. Margie kept the note and handed her husband the paper. His eyes boggled at the headline and then wandered to the war souvenirs he'd mounted on the wall—his grandfather's rapier from the Napoleonic Wars, his uncle's cap from British India, an Damascene sword his father snatched during a battle in Egypt, and a silk board pinned with medals. His chest swelled with pride. Although he had missed a chance to serve God and King, his own son would soon march off to battle, sure to return victorious and with treasures of his own to mount on the wall. He wiped his eyes and returned to the table to cut into his tomato. The red juice ran into the orange bubbles of grease, which he mopped up with the toast and washed down with coffee.

Outside, a parade was stirring. Just like in Leamington, people in the surrounding villages of Blackdown, Offchurch, Clubbington and a thousand others across the land paraded down the streets, walking or riding and waving the Union Jack for all to see. Young boys ran along the parade route and wrestled with each other, while older ones stared up at propaganda posters, confused at what they saw and what it meant for them. Beggars asked around for the locations of recruitment offices. Mothers and daughters huddled together, realizing it could be the last days they would spend with their fathers and brothers. Factories rolled out guns, ammunition, and artillery shells that clinked together like heavy coins. And from the woods and plains of Warwickshire, to the lakes and the bleak highlands up north, and to the chalk cliffs of Dover down south, every part of England echoed the same refrain: England at War with Germany! And across the waters that tossed black and cold with *unterseeboots* lurking in the deep, hundreds of thousands of the Belgian elderly and the children and the wealthy made their way to hospitals and schools and brothels and other shelters where they could take cover from the German artillery. They left their lives behind, while soldiers bled out in their beds, used their kitchens and toilets, slaughtered their livestock, and dug trenches through their ancestors' graves.

~ CONSTANCE BAKER ~

Watching Luther roll truffles was like, I don't know, maybe like watching a monk pray. Yes. Like that. Luther was a monk, chocolate was his religion, and the truffles he created were his prayer beads.

Before he started, he was no different than the other chefs. He melted the chocolate over boiling water, lightly mixed in the crème, and stirred until his eyes narrowed. But then everything changed. Once he reached into that bowl to start rolling the chocolate globes between his palms, his eyes emptied and his body acted on its own accord. He rocked back and forth on his heels as he worked, lips slightly parted. He was a force of nature, a river flowing unrelentingly to the sea. A breeze ruffled his hair, a bee buzzed by and landed on his arm, a rival baker dropped a pan and let out a string of hushed curses, but Luther did not waver. I'd look away and he'd already have ten truffles done.

Other chefs stared at us from their tents, red-faced, running hands through their hair, shouting orders to their various apprentices. Luther, by himself, had already covered his table in truffles.

In front of the individual contestant's tents, spectators and judges watched from rows of white garden chairs. They whispered to one another and nodded at Luther, ignoring the other chefs. One of the judges glanced down and flipped open his great, silver pocket watch.

"Chefs be warned, five minutes remain on the clock," he announced.

Luther didn't look up from his work. He had covered two tables with truffles.

The other chefs panicked.

"Forget the ganache, Matthew, there's no time! Help me plate the truffles!"

Just before the judge called time, Luther selected a set of perfect truffles and with lightning-fast fingers, arranged them on his favorite display plate. It was a work of art. And by the time the judge called time, Luther had three tables of truffles. He took a step back, smiled at the audience, and held up his arms. That was his trademark, and the audience responded with their polite little finger-claps.

The judge held up his bullhorn and called out, "Please observe a one-hour judging period."

Slowly, the audience stood and conversation rose, like an intermission.

"Great job, love." I kissed Luther on the cheek and rubbed his back.

He smiled his wide-dimpled smile and flapped his hands. Suddenly, he realized what he was doing and stuck his hands in his pockets. I didn't even have to tell him anymore.

"Did you see how many I made?"

"Yeah, but don't start bragging. Nobody likes a bragger, remember that."

"Why don't people like braggers?"

"They talk about how they're better than everyone else."

"Yeah, but why do they talk about how they're better than everyone else?"

"I don't know. It's because they don't believe in themselves, I guess."

"Yeah, but why don't they believe in themselves?"

"I'll tell you later," I said, knowing we'd both forget in ten minutes.

From afar, I noticed three women from the audience walking up toward our tent. All dressed up in lovely floral dresses and fancy hats, they were probably related to some earl or minor royalty. They carried umbrellas. Umbrellas. On a warm sunny day in the middle of summer. As they drew closer, I could tell they were in their twenties—probably close to Luther's age. The smile dropped from my face, and I put my guard up.

"Are you Luther?" one of them asked, "The No-trifle Truffler? The Mozart of Marzipan?"

He nodded, face red. They giggled to each other.

"What do you want?" I asked. They frowned at my bluntness, but I would not allow Luther to be toyed with.

They exchanged glances and, then one of the girls said, "We only wanted to ask Luther about his baking. We go to your sweet shop all the time. We love it."

Paying customers. Posh customers. But I didn't recognize them and said so. "Well, that's lovely to hear, but I afraid to say I don't recognize you. Luther and I work very hard to make sure everyone enjoys our sweets, and we always try to remember our frequent customers."

One of the girls, the one who looked to be the leader of their little pack, spoke up. "Oh, well, we do love your sweets, but it's usually one of the kitchen staff that actually goes to the shop. You see, I am a ward of Lord Brooke, the Earl of Warwick, and I've been staying at the castle. Cook tells me that our dessert chef is nearing retirement age, and we"—she looked at Luther—"she is looking for a new one. And we thought, well, isn't there a famous baker right in our back yard?"

I gasped. I couldn't help it. A job? A job for Luther? If I could get him to be self-sustaining, to take care of himself so I wouldn't have to worry about him when I'm gone...

She turned to Luther. "Of course, Chef would have to give you a proper interview, but we've all tasted your work. Even Chef says its very good and she does love her sweets." The other girls laughed and commented on Chef's sweet tooth.

My life would be complete. I'd always planned for Jim to take over the store and take care of his brother, but that didn't work out. Now, if Luther had a real job, I could get struck by lightning tomorrow and it wouldn't matter, so long as he could support himself. But, wait. What if it didn't work out? What if dealing with strange people in a strange kitchen would be too much for him? Would he be able to handle himself away from me?

"We would love the opportunity," I finally said, slowly. "Luther is, after all, the best candy maker in central England. And he loves to try new recipes and create new desserts. I don't think you could find a better person for the job."

"Good." The girl turned to Luther. "How would you like to work in the castle, Luther?"

"The castle? I would like that."

She smiled up at him. "Excellent. You should stop by the castle next Monday at at 10 o'clock sharp. Go around back to the kitchen entry and ask for Chef. There will be an interview of sorts, but I think it's probably only a formality."

Luther looked at me and then back at the girls. "Thank you," he said. "I like candy very much."

With that, the girls floated back over to the audience, where they joined their friends.

Luther won the contest. It was his tenth blue ribbon, and no one was surprised when they called his name and passed out his truffles for everyone to eat. That was mostly what they came for—the hundreds of truffles they knew Luther would make. I hid the prize money in my slip, and we took the train back home to Leamington.

On the train, I resolved that Luther needed to take the job. It would probably be the only job offer he would ever receive. I knew they would provide him with room and board, but would they be nice to him? What if something happened that he couldn't deal with? I pictured him flapping his hands and running around the formal dining room while the Earl of Warwick looked on in horror. But maybe since Warwick wasn't far from Leamington Spa, he could live at home and bike to the castle every morning.

"How do you feel about working in the castle?" I asked.

"I don't know." He stuck his hands in his pocket again and looked away.

"Yes, you do. Spit it out, I won't get mad."

"What if they're mean to me?"

I put my arm around him, and he hugged me. I felt his his heart thud in his chest. A full-grown man, twenty-six years old, still curling up next to his Mum. Even if I could, I wouldn't have changed a thing about him.

"There will always be mean people," I said. "Some will disguise their meanness with big ideas, like politics or business or economics or whatever else. But they don't last. They never do."

"Why don't they last?"

"Because goodness always wins in the end." At least that's what I'd been trying to tell myself these last few years. "And if you have an idea as small and tender as a crumb and you hide it inside your heart, nobody can take it away. They'll might try to reach inside you and drag it out—" I poked him in the chest. He laughed. "But it will be so small, you see, that it will always slip through their fingers."

When the train arrived at the station back home, we were surprised at all the activity. We carried our suitcases down the street, and right away I noticed the giant signs with blue and red lettering.

ENGLAND EXPECTS EVERY MAN TO DO HIS DUTY. JOIN THE ARMY TODAY.

As soon as we unpacked our suitcases, Luther and I headed over to Lavinia's. On our way, we passed the crowd of boys and young men standing in front of Carraway's Pub, which now boasted a sign that said "Recruiting Office." It made sense that old Mr. Carraway, the veteran that he was, would be eager to loan his place of business to the army.

At Lavinia's, she ushered us into the drawing room and poured tea.

"Have you read the news??" she asked.

"No. Honestly, we were so busy with the contest and it seemed so far away until now."

"Germany demanded passage through Belgium, and they refused, so Germany declared war and invaded. Under the Treaty of London, we're obligated to join the fray to protect Belgium. Now, it seems the whole world is on fire!"

"What about Mark?"

Lavinia's back straightened. "Mark's a man of peace, which is why I love him so. Some ladies gave him the white feather yesterday, but he doesn't care. He said the postal service is reorganizing for the war with the Royal Engineers. It means he'll be doing his duty sorting letters to and from the soldiers, probably in London."

We were both quiet for a moment as we sipped our tea.

"London's not too far," I said. "It's better than a battlefield."

She nodded, took a sip, and then looked at me. "Have you heard anything from Jim?"

I could feel my own back straighten and the color rise in my cheeks. "You know how I feel about Jim." I tried to keep my voice even. "He turned his back on this family when he left school and disappeared. Sending word now and again about a job here or there does not make up for that."

Lavinia sighed. I knew she still had a soft spot for Jim. "So you haven't heard anything at all?"

"No." I'd flipped through the mail when we returned home, but there was nothing. I wasn't even going to confess that I looked for a note. I told myself since the war had broken out, maybe he'd write to say he'd enlisted, finally done something right. But, no. Nothing. "But I have news about Luther," I said to change the subject. "He's gone and got himself a job offer. At Warwick Castle, no less."

"Luther!" Lavinia squealed with delight and gave him a big hug. "You are full of surprises!"

We chatted about the castle and what working there might be like and then Lavinia suggested we stay for dinner. Mark would be working late at the post office helping to get things organized for the war effort, and I could tell Lavinia didn't want to be alone.

"I'm a terrible hostess, though. I'm afraid I'm out of everything. I don't think I've been to the market since all this started."

"No matter, we can all walk down together. We still have the whole afternoon."

Lavinia smiled. "Then it's settled. I'll get my hat."

On the way to the market, we had to pass the recruiting office, and I could tell all the hubbub set Luther ill at ease. As we wandered the aisles, he followed along picking up fruits and vegetables as if feeling them in his hands grounded him amidst all the noise and excitement. Lavinia and I planned a shepherd's pie and gathered all the ingredients, plus a few extra staples we both needed. While I was at the potato stand, I suddenly realized Luther wasn't behind me. I turned around and couldn't see Luther anywhere.

I grabbed Lavinia's arm. "Where's Luther?"

She looked around as if suddenly noticing he'd gone missing. "I don't know. He was here just a moment ago."

My heart thudded in my chest even though I tried to reassure myself. "He's probably gone to the baking aisle." When Luther was younger, I would never dream of taking him to the market. There was simply too much noise and activity and colors. Too many people. The few times I did take him ended in a minor disaster. But after he discovered the truffles, everything had changed. Now he usually went to the market with me and, although he stayed close, I knew he was more at ease, people knew him, and he never made any trouble. Yes, I told myself, he's probably just over checking the price of sugar and flour.

~ LUTHER BAKER ~

I saw the apples down the aisle from where Mum was looking at potatoes to make the dinner pie and the apples looked good to eat so I went to look at them. But I didn't eat the apples because Mum always told me not to take anything because stealing was bad. I tried it once and people yelled at me and I got in trouble so I didn't take the apples. But the apples were so red and I knew how juicy and crunchy they would be if I bit them with my teeth. I could almost taste the apple and I started to pick one up but then remembered not to and that's when Mr. Stoker came up and said I will buy an apple for you. Mr. Stoker was happy and shook my hand and he had a hard handshake and dry hands and I don't know why. I said I'm not sure if I should eat the apple because Mum wouldn't want me to and I got in trouble before but he told me it wasn't stealing because yes he was going to buy it for me. That was a nice thing to do. Yes please I said and he bought me an apple and I ate it. I told him I couldn't find Mum because I turned around and she was not there.

Mr. Stoker said he will take me to Mum and I said thank you and you are being very nice. I wonder why. Mr. Stoker told me he heard about my awards I got for making candy and said he was very proud of me and I said thank you but I didn't brag because Mum told me nobody likes people who brag about things they do because they act like they are better than everyone else because they don't believe in themselves. That's what I told him. Mr. Stoker smiled and asked about Jim I told him Jim went to a school where they learn things but he didn't finish school and is living in a town somewhere but I dod't know where but I miss him because he always took care of me and Mr. Stoker told me how Jim always got in trouble when he was a kid and how he was a bad friend for Rodney and made Rodney do bad things to get him in trouble. Mr. Stoker asked me if Jim got in trouble with Mum a lot and I said I don't know but I was really thinking about all the times Jim and Mum fought with each other and got mad. Mr. Stoker asked if I remembered hitting Rodney. I said I don't know because Mum told me never to tell anyone about it or I would get in trouble. Mr. Stoker said Jim was a bad brother for me and that Jim did not know how to be a man and that he tried to help Jim become a good man but could not help him be a good man. I didn't know. He said he wanted to help me be a good man and teach me to stand up for others and help the country and one day have a family that would be nice for the God and the King. He asked me if I wanted to do that. I said I don't know. He said don't be shy now and I said I guess and he said he would help me do that and he walked me to the line of boys standing in the street all lined up in front of a door. I asked why they were lined up and Mr. Stoker said it was because they were going to help the country and become men like he said I said I wanted to. He said I said I wanted to become a man and help. I asked how were they helping and he said the country was fighting an army that was killing people. I said that was sad and asked if they would hurt Mum and Jim and Mr. Stoker said yes it is sad and they will hurt everyone if we don't stop them including Mum and Jim. He said if I wanted to protect them like a man I would sign up to be a soldier. I didn't know what Mum would say to that and looked around but he said I could go back if I wanted but look at the big crowd of boys lined up here to do the right thing and be men and they all looked at me and I didn't want them to look at me because there were too many of them. Mr. Stoker said I could turn back any time I wanted but there were too many people so I asked will you take me back to Mum and he said as soon as I signed my name to the paper he would take me back to Mum and she would be proud of me so I stood in line even though I don't know how to write my name on the paper and the room was so full and there were too many people so I wanted to write my name on the papers so Mum would be proud of me and I could go find her and so Mr. Stoker helped me go to the front of the line where there was a man who asked me questions like my name and where my dad was born. I said I didn't know my dad and he asked me how old I was and if I was married and my job. I said I made sweets for the sweet shop but that I was going to get a new job and make sweets in the castle and they said not anymore. Some of the questions I didn't know, so Mr. Stoker whispered me the answer in my ear and then they measured how tall I was and asked me to cover my eye and look at something. Then I was supposed to write my name on a paper but I said I couldn't write my name so Mr. Stoker wrote my name for me and the man said it was okay because he made two shillings and sixpence per recruit. Then I had to put my hand on a Bible and repeat after what the man said and then it was done and I was a man who helped the country and I was happy how I was finished and it was time to go find Mum and she would be proud of me. But Mr. Stoker laughed and said he didn't know where Mum was so I had to go find her myself.

~ CONSTANCE BAKER ~

"*What the hell did you do to my son?*" I'd pushed and shoved my way through the line of soon-to-be soldiers filling the street in front of the pub, and marched up to the desk of the recruiting officer.

"I asked you a question! What the hell did you do to my son?"

The man opened his mouth, but no words came out.

"You just signed up Luther Baker. Show me his papers."

He finally found his voice. "I can't do that. The papers are confidential," he said quietly.

"How much money do you want? Just name it; I will give you anything."

"I repeat. The papers are confidential."

"Do you have a wife? A child? Someone you must protect at all costs?" I demanded.

"Madam—" He stood up.

With a sweep of my arm, I knocked all the hundreds of neatly stacked documents off his desk and sent them fluttering to the ground. All noise of conversation from the crowd of young boys at the door immediately died down.

"*Enough!*" Father Carmichael's voice sounded from the door. The old man entered with a parcel under his arm. He must have been on his way to the post office. Lavinia was with him. "What in the world is happening here? Mrs. Baker, explain yourself."

"They tricked him into enlisting!"

"Tricked who?" Then his eyes widened in understanding. "Luther?"

I nodded, unable to speak. Lavinia wrapped an arm around my shoulder.

"God in heaven. What is wrong with you?" Father Carmichael approached the recruiting officer.

"What's the problem, Father? I've enlisted dozens of young men today alone. For the defense of our country."

"Yes, but Luther isn't right in the head. Everyone in Leamington Spa knows that." Father Carmichael said, trying to take a diplomatic approach to the problem. "He would never qualify to be a soldier. Why sometimes he can barely even talk, let alone follow orders. It's best you correct this mistake before your senior officers find out."

"Well, if he can't follow orders, then … yes." The man looked at me. "I apologize, ma'am."

"Just find his papers and tear them up." I choked out, then watched him bend down to find the correct paper.

"Stand down, soldier!" A voice called from the entrance. Mr. Stoker.

I turned slowly, as if time itself had had fallen away and all that remained was fear. And disbelief. And *rage*.

"We must maintain the strictest discipline when it comes to military matters," Mr. Stoker announced, striding through the crowd as if he was the prime minister himself. "I understand that a priest—a man of God—and a worried mother might oppose sending a young man to war, but no one is exempt from making sacrifices to protect the nation. And, Father Carmichael, I'm sure you will agree that this is a matter of state, not for the church to interfere."

Father Carmichael looked down at the recruiter. "Luther could very well be a danger to his fellows if he's sent to the front. You could be putting other boys in harm's way if you don't tear that paper up." The recruiter looked up at the priest and then redoubled his search for Luther's paper. Father Carmichael drew himself to his full height and turned to Mr. Stoker. "And you jolly well know Luther is in no way prepared to fight on behalf of our country."

"I know nothing of the sort," Mr. Stoker sneered. "He can carry a rifle the same as any of these boys," He turned and swept his arm out to indicate the room full of gawking boys. Then he turned and looked straight at me. "I daresay Luther can *push* his way through the ranks if need be."

My knees buckled and my sight narrowed until all I could see was Stoker's smirk. Lavinia's grip was the only reason I remained upright. And then the recruiting officer found Luther's paper and held it up.

"Here it is," he said and scrambled to his feet and then started to rip the paper in two.

"Not so fast." Mr. Stoker now stood directly in front of the recruiter. He held his hand out to take Luther's paper.

The recruiter looked to Father Carmichael, then to me. He hesitated.

Stoker cleared his throat and leaned forward. "Surely you don't want to jeopardize your career." His voice was a quiet menace. "I will be forced to report your actions if you neglect your duty and turn away a willing, able-bodied young man. Despite what this priest says, Luther *is* able bodied and, therefore, *is* able to serve. Now, I want to see you gather up all those papers and get them submitted. Come, let's not make a scene of it."

That was it. I struggled free of Lavinia and reached for Luther's paper, but Father Carmichael grabbed my arm.

"Don't interfere, Mrs. Baker. Perhaps there's another way. I will make an appeal up the chain of command."

"This can't be happening! Don't let them take him away!" I struggled to break free from Father Carmichael, but he held me tight.

"Take heart, Mrs. Baker," Stoker said looking down at me. "Your feminine emotions and attempt to shield your son have long clouded your thinking. Luther will do his duty and pay the price for freedom. As we all must."

I was vaguely aware of the recruiter as he gathered the rest of the papers from the floor, stuffed them in an envelope and dropped them into a locked box on his desk.

It was over. Luther was going to war.

~ LAVINIA BELL ~

Luther didn't understand what was happening when they put him on that train. As the boys lined up and their names were called, he kept asking when he could make truffles again and why wasn't his mother getting on the train with him and were they going to another baking contest? And then when the train left the station, it was like Constance's spirit left, too. She made herself smile and kiss Luther goodbye, and I don't know how she held it together as I was crying so hard I could barely see.

I had watched the world treat my sister unfairly for so many years. I had watched her fights with our mum when Mum had too much to drink and lashed out, had watched her fret when she realized Luther was not like other boys, had watched her mourn when James died, had watched her do everything she could to keep running the shop while caring for Luther and putting all her hopes and dreams and aspirations on little Jim. While others talked behind her back, I had tried to shield her, help her, protect her. But now it was like she was all emptied out. Mum had lashed out at her, then Father, who had tried to protect us, died. James, who loved her so completely, had died too young. Luther had tried her patience. Jim had abandoned her. Stoker had betrayed her. And now Luther was gone and there was nothing I could do to fix it.

I tried to tell her that Father Carmichael had written to someone in London to tell them about Luther's problems and about his talent as a baker. He hoped maybe he'd be stationed at some general's headquarters making truffles for senior staffers rather than carrying a rifle in some trench somewhere. But with Mr. Stoker's connections, I held out little hope. He had obviously nurtured his grudge against Luther all these years and had seen his chance for revenge. And now Constance held out no hope at all.

After the train left, I followed Constance to the cemetery on the edge of town, where she knelt at her husband's grave. I don't think she'd been there in twenty years.

Oh James. What would her life had been like if he had lived? Jim had been a constant reminder of his father—he looked just like him—but caring for Luther alone had been the biggest burden of James's death and a constant reminder for Constance of what she had lost.

Of the life she might have had.

She said nothing at the graveside and then said nothing as she rose and walked back to the house. The shop was dark. The house was empty. And so it remained for many weeks after.

August ended with high enthusiasm for the war, and it was the only thing anyone would talk about. Constance had finally opened the store again, but because sugar and milk was rationed, it was hard to get supplies enough to make big batches of anything. He heart wasn't in baking anyway. The only times she ventured out was to buy groceries, and the customers who did stop by noticed the corners of the shop were dark and dusty.

The bell above the door would tinkle and a customer would enter and see her at the counter, head rested on her palm, leafing through the paper but not reading it. *One toffee, please,* they might ask. *That'll be sixpence,* she would reply. *Yes, here it is, thank you.* And the customer would leave, bell tinkling behind them.

September and October were the same. Everything was the same—monotonous, thoughtless. I noticed how she would forget things, like how much sugar she needed to buy or how much flour to add to her recipes. Ethyl Brand, the sweet little girl who once played the piano at my wedding, now twenty-three and studying to become a nun, started visiting. She and Constance would speak, but I know not what of.

Town had emptied out, and the only men left behind were too young, too old, too infirm, or too posh like Mr. Stoker, God forgive him.

Mark was working at a post depot in London, and we wrote to each other every day. Sometimes I went down to visit. He joked that he handled my letters in the bin at work while he was sorting and, being a postman, took the liberty to deliver his own post to himself.

Sometimes I wrote to Jim. Constance would not hear a word about him and refused to ask after him. I thought he might've enlisted, but he said he had a factory job making guns in Birmingham and that he had a flat there. I thought maybe I would go see him one day. He never forgave his mother for sending him away and she never forgave him for leaving school. Both were too stubborn to make amends, but Jim and I had always been close, and I hoped someday things would change between mother and son.

I couldn't believe he was grown already. Every day I felt myself becoming an old woman. I rose in the morning stiff and cold, seeing in the mirror the silver strands of hair that appeared suddenly at my temple. The years were passing so quickly. First, I'd come to Leamington Spa for Constance, then I became a young wife, and, unable to have children of my own, I helped raise Luther and Jim. I do not believe I succeeded.

I approached every day with the gentle step of a kindly granny, half out of the fear that I was becoming old and needed to act the part, half out of the guilt that comes with making it this far when so many others had paid a higher price during the war—or paid the ultimate price.

I thought to myself, *I will write again to Jim. I will ask him to come home. And if he says no, I will go visit him, too.*

~ CONSTANCE BAKER ~

The lights were out in Baker's Sweets. Fingerprints smeared the toffee jars. The pink wallpaper and cherry-stained shelves had aged grey with dust and scuff marks; they hadn't been scrubbed in weeks. The ledger book sat on the counter next to a cup of cold coffee.

Today's Sales:

A single period sat on the line where I had pressed pencil to paper, paused, and then put the pencil back in the drawer.

Upstairs, I got getting ready for bed. Still wearing the day's clothes, I sat heavily on the mattress. The springs squeaked. I untied my apron strings, flung the flour-stained garment over the end of the bed post and watched it float to the ground, where it landed on top of a pile of dirty clothes littering the floor. An old book on business management lay half buried under last week's cardigans, a book James had loved. I'd always meant to read it; I had begun to read it a dozen times. Perhaps I could do a bit of reading before turning out the light. But then, like every other night for the past few months, I decided against it. I glanced at the drawn curtains and entertained the idea of looking down on the street before bed—maybe the rain had finally turned to snow—but decided against that, too. I leaned back on my pillow and stared up at the ceiling. *Where are you, Luther? Please be safe. Please, God, let him be safe.*

Knock! Knock! Knock!

My eyes flew open. *Somebody's at the door. Something's happened to Luther!*

Knock! Knock! Knock!

No. They wouldn't come to deliver bad news this time of night. If I ignore it, they'll bugger off. I shut my eyes again.

Knock! Knock! Knock!

Yawning, I pulled my cardigan off of the floor and descended the steps, bare feet on cold wood.

Knock! Knock! Knock!

A man was at the door, cap down over his forehead, cupping his hands around his eyes to see through the glass panes, nostril fumes fogging the glass.

"Mum!" the man called, "Mum!"

"Luther," I breathed.

I fumbled with the jingling keys, threw open the door, and pulled him in for a hug before anyone could take him away again. And then I stopped. Luther should've been taller than me.

"You're not my son." I tightened my grip on his hands. The cricket bat was at the other end of the room—too far away to grab. My words seemed to shut him up. He was unshaven—a woolen brown fuzz softened his chin and jaw.

"Oh, come, now, Mum. You know me." He gave a weak smile and reached out to finish the hug. I held up an arm, stopping him. By the yellow light of the electrical street lamps that glared through the shop window, I noticed his knuckles were red and blotchy. I touched them. He knit his brow.

"How?"

"Factory laid me off—roughhousing during work hours or something like that—but it's not important. Lavinia wrote and told me what happened to Luther."

Lavinia. He used to call her Auntie Lavinia. Now he calls her Lavinia.

"You're three months late."

"I've been busy."

"You've been getting drunk and street brawling, that's what you've been busy with. You're an irresponsible child."

He rolled his eyes and laughed. "I don't even get a hug?"

He said it like it was a joke, like I was required to hug my son after he dropped out of school, wasting my hard-earned money so he could wallow from slum to slum and job to job.

"No."

He looked at the ground, and the smile left him.

"You're here for a job, aren't you? You have nowhere else to turn, so you're back here as a last resort."

Jim's eyes roved around the shop taking in the empty display cases, the unswept floor, the unopened mail. Judging it, like he had a right to judge anything. With his shoe, he toed today's mail, still on the floor where it had fallen through the slot. He raised his brow at me when he saw a letter from the government that I refused to open.

"I've not been good to you, Mum," he muttered. "I know I wasted your money with school and all—"

"I worked myself raw for that tuition," I whispered, voice shaking. "I put all my hopes and dreams in you and you couldn't even—"

"Lavinia tells me you could use some help around here."

"Not from you. Never from you."

He opened his mouth.

"Get out," my voice cracked, and I was afraid I'd start yelling. Or weeping. "Just get out. I won't put my faith in you again."

Some valve inside him must've broke because his face flushed red and hot. I didn't care. I shut the door in my son's face, locked it, then wandered to the kitchen, stepping over a pile of newspapers. I cleared an empty sack—not sure what it was doing there—off of my chair at the kitchen table and sat. Propping my face on my palm, I stared at the table while the soft rain whispered on the siding and the wood beams creaked overhead. Those beams were from the 1700s when the Baker family built the house—three stories of Georgian terrace that had seen plenty of happiness and plenty of sadness in its time. Especially sadness. And loss.

Jim. *Jim*. He thought that I needed his help. Thought that since he was grown man, he could take care of himself, while I was some weak old lady. But all he knew how to do was mess up. And refuse. Refuse everything

I'd ever offered him. He couldn't tell me a single thing in this world he actually wanted, yet was so quick to refuse a life, a family, this house, the whole shop. Jesus Christ, he was still the same six-year-old boy who fought—and lost to—just about every other boy in town. He made it his duty to retaliate against everyone who made fun of Luther until the only thing the boy knew was fighting, playing at fighting, and being angry. I thought sending him away to school would put him on the right path, but I was wrong. Seems like with Jim, I was always wrong.

I sat that way most of the night, my thoughts running in circles, always coming back to my youngest son. My chest tightened until it hurt, and I wanted to hit something, to break something. But I didn't. Eventually, I fell asleep. It was an angry, hot-blooded kind of sleep. I dreamed Jim died of a heart attack, and I went to his funeral with Lavinia and the Prime Minister, and we laid him down in the earth next to his father and Luther, who was already dead and gone. An unusual dream, no doubt; some might think it disturbing, even. I cried in it, cried till I had no more tears left, but when I woke, my eyes were dry.

~ JIM BAKER ~

*I*t's alright. It's alright; doesn't bother me a bit. I'm fine. When people wrong me, I get back at them. I always did, and I always will. That was me—calm, cold, and savvy, witty even, when the whole world was on fire. What was she thinking, refusing my help? She was proud, too proud. Couldn't admit she was a wreck and had been a wreck ever since Luther left. God damn Stoker, thinking he could fool Luther like that. I took a piss on their front door sometime around midnight, hoped he'd enjoy that.

Then I tried for Lavinia's house, where I was pretty sure I'd get a warmer greeting. I knocked on the door, but no one answered. Sleeping, no doubt. I kept knocking, *rap rap rap rap rapping* on the wood for about a minute. I knocked with varying intensity, trying to avoid periodic sounds a sleeping person might mistake for beams creaking in the wind. Finally, footsteps sounded inside. I pressed my face to the glass and looked through the cracks between the curtains. Inside was the floral sofa, the coffee table, the radio, and the kitchen table through the doorway in the far back of the house. I gave a rapid-fire knocking. Finally, a lightbulb flashed in one of the upstairs windows. I stepped back from the door, smoothed my hair, and cleared my throat.

The doorknob clicked, and the door swung inward. I started to smile but then frowned when I didn't see Lavinia there.

"Hey, Mark."

"Jim? That you? You in trouble? It's late."

Mark yawned, setting down his cricket bat.

"So tell me, does everyone in Leamington Spa answer the door with a cricket bat?" I chuckled.

He tilted his head, confused.

"Can I come in?"

"Is it just you?"

"Yeah, of course."

What kind of question is that?

I stepped inside, out of the rain. An orange ember sat in the hearth under the ashes, and I smelled coal. Mark motioned toward the couch, and I took a seat on the cushions I had napped on so many times in my youth.

"You home for good?"

I nodded. "Heard you've been at work in London for a while."

"Still am." He rubbed his neck. "Every once in a while, I get a day or two off to visit home. They're decent folk."

"I haven't met too many of those."

I noticed Mark was wearing a woman's bathrobe—satin, pastel green. Must've been so tired he grabbed Lavinia's on the way down.

"You're too hard on folks, Jim. Especially yourself," Mark said. "Did you lose another job?"

"Lavinia suggested I come home and help out Mum." Then, in a quieter tone, "And yes, I'm also out of a job."

"Well, I'm sure Lavinia will be happy to see you."

"Is she not here?"

"No, she's here."

"Well, I'm anxious to see her, too." I looked around.

"Please, Jim, it's," he squinted at the clock over the mantle, "a quarter after midnight."

"Oh yeah, of course. My mistake. I'm sorry."

"You can sleep on the sofa for tonight. She'll see you in the morning. Hungry? Thirsty?"

"Yeah, have anything to drink?"

"Water."

"No thanks."

"But you just said you were thirsty."

"Changed my mind."

Mark shrugged. He went to the linen closet, pulled out a few blankets, set them down for me on the sofa, and tiptoed back up the stairs. He left the cricket bat beside the door.

So that's it? A fine welcome for the prodigal son.

Popping my shoes off, I lay down on the sofa. The springs squeaked under me. It was nice, really, like when I was kid. I looked around the room at the familiar pictures—etchings of great-grandparents, blotchy wedding photographs that had been colorized with fake rosy cheeks and a blue sky. I found myself standing in the background, a dark-eyed five-year-old standing next to ... Ethyl Brand? Wow. I looked pretty good as a five-year-old. And so did she.

When I opened my eyes, the light shined gold over the Georgian eaves. The little row houses on the cobblestone were darkened by last night's shower.

"Jim? Jim?" A familiar voice came from the top of the stairs, and I heard rushed footsteps on the wood steps.

There was Aunt Lavinia in her satin bathrobe, arms stretched out. She rushed over and covered me in a hug, warm and soft.

"My prodigal nephew has returned!" She kissed my forehead. "Slaughter the fatted calf."

She took me into the kitchen, where Mark soon joined us. Together, they made a quick breakfast by cracking three eggs on the pan, throwing in sliced tomato, and putting on a kettle for coffee. The plates and forks and cups clacked as we pulled open drawers and cupboards, and soon we were at the table. Mark ate quickly, swallowing his whole coffee in two takes.

"Have to get to the station for an early train. Got to be in London by noon. Sorry I can't stay too long, Jim."

"It's alright. Thanks for letting me sleep on the couch."

"So what are your plans for today?" Lavinia asked me. "Have you spoken with your mother yet?"

"Eeh, I'll tell you about that later. Right now, I'm just looking for work, I guess."

"Shouldn't be too hard," Mark mumbled. "Plenty of factory jobs nowadays for making bombs and bullets."

I shrugged. Bombs and bullets were not my favorite things.

"What kind of job do you want?" Lavinia asked, picking a forkful of egg from Mark's plate. He smiled at her and touched her hand. Still fond of each other after all these years. Amazing.

"What kind of job? Hmm ... how about high pay, low hours, where I don't have to talk to anyone, yet I get lots of credit."

"Doesn't sound like any job I know," Mark laughed. "How about the REPS?"

"The what?"

"The Royal Engineers Postal Service. We handle all the mail to and from the front. They're always hiring, and plenty of local mailmen get picked up by them. I'd put in a word for you."

"I'd have to work with people?"

"It takes lots of people to sort the volume of mail we handle. It's often solitary work, but yes, there are lots of us on the job."

"That's alright."

Mark shifted in his seat and looked at me. "Why not? I'm basically guaranteeing you a job."

"I can't explain it. I just don't like people."

"Alright, then," Mark said, leaning back in his chair.

We returned to eating in quiet. I had just finished my egg when Mark piped up again.

"Forgive me if I'm wrong, but—"

"You're wrong."

He continued. "I think you want people to turn up their noses at you."

Who is this guy—Sigmund Freud?

I ignored him and continued eating. Pretty soon he checked the clock.

"Oh, time to go." He grabbed his coat and put on his hat. He gave me a curt nod and kissed Lavinia on the cheek. "Till next time, dear." Then he closed the door behind him and the house was quiet.

"Well," Lavinia said after a moment, "now that we're alone, you simply must tell me about your mother. And I won't take no for an answer."

"It's nothing terrible. I just stopped by the house last night, and she was pretty upset. She's definitely not interested in my helping in the shop and—"

My throat closed on its own accord, and I couldn't speak all of a sudden. I cleared my throat to make it look like an intentional cough. It was strange because I swear I wasn't sad; my body was acting for me. Blinking a few times, I picked at the threads of the table cloth and then looked out the window, away from my aunt.

"I'm sorry to hear it. Did you make your case?"

"I tried to apologize."

"It's much too late for that." She shook her head, stirring her tea. "You need to actually *do* something. You might not ever be able to recreate the sweet shop in all of its glory, but you can at least recreate your family."

"You think I should get married? Because I don't have much a history with women."

"Jim, I asked you to come back because your family needs you. Is that why you're here, or is it just because you got yourself fired again, and you've nowhere else to go?"

The words came out quickly with clipped consonants.

I paused. That was not the Aunt Lavinia I remembered. I set my napkin on the table and stood. "I have to go look for a job. Thank you for breakfast."

Lavinia opened her mouth to speak but said nothing. Instead, her tongue clicked on the roof of her mouth. I grabbed my coat to leave.

"Fine. You get your job, Jim, and when you get it, half the money is going to your mother."

"She wouldn't take it," I chuckled, "I can see it now—"

Quick as a flash, Aunt Lavinia was out of her chair with a pointed finger in my face. "You shut your mouth about your mum," she hissed. "Last three months, I've watched my sister turn into a recluse. She sits in that dark house all day with no one. She's lost her husband, one of her sons is at war, and the other wants nothing to do with her *even* after all she tried to give him every opportunity."

I felt myself shrink back, my mind go blank. She had scared all of my thoughts away, and all I could do was look at her. I'd had everyone else yell at me, but now Aunt Lavinia?

"She's dying inside, Jim." She smack her hand on the table, probably wishing it could've been the side of my head. "Leave your resentment in the past and stop behaving like you're six years old."

"Yes ma'am," I said quietly.

"You're a grown man. It's past time for you to act like one."

I left the house with a somber step. It was about 9 o'clock, and the day's business was just beginning. First thing, I walked to Bath Street, where I turned left. I kept my hands in my pockets and my collar up against the cold. There was the paper boy on his bicycle, delivering the Leamington Courier. Paper boy didn't sound like too hard of a job; an hour or so of work each morning, and I'd have a little pocket change. I added that to my list. Well, I didn't have an actual list with me, so I just remembered it. I put it on my mental list, how's that?

Midway through the street was my house. Three stories of Georgian façade—six windows, ground floor with glazed white brick. The discolored wood ran around the shop window, where we'd show off our twelve flavours of bonbons, each one with its own jar. *Baker's Sweets*, said the faded letters just above the window. I peeked inside; nobody was at the counter. I touched the doorknob, turning it so slowly that nobody would hear the *click*, and then pushed door open slowly, inch by inch, so the bells wouldn't jingle. I was a professional; I'd done this hundreds of times as a boy. Once inside, I stepped over the squeaky floorboard, over to the jar of bonbons. Looking around, I slipped a hand in and pulled out a handful of the little pink pebbles, dusted in flour and sugar. I fit one in my mouth and pressed my teeth into its soft chocolate shell. There was that familiar chocolate-coconut paste that I had to work my jaw for. Just like Mum always made it.

I had no idea where she'd gone out to, but I figured she'd be back soon. I could've slipped right back out the front door, but instead found myself wandering toward the kitchen. I saw the unopened pile of mail, now on the kitchen table. *Hmm.* The letter from the government was still there. Had she even looked at them?

His Britannic Majesty's Government

Interesting. Postmarked from London in late October, I picked it up, sliced open with my pinky, pulled out the contents, and unfolded the slip of paper.

HER ROYAL HIGHNESS PRINCESS MARY'S SAILORS' AND SOLDIERS' CHRISTMAS FUNDSEEKING CONTRIBUTIONS FROM INDEPENDENT SWEETS PRODUCERS

Dear Sir,

This Christmas, Her Royal Highness Princess Mary will endeavor to send more than two million Christmas tins to the soldiers, sailors, nurses, and other military personnel who have put themselves at risk for the defense of our homeland. The tins will contain an assortment of gifts, such as cigarettes, tobacco, stationery, and sweets. As the project is privately funded, donations are always needed. However, Princess Mary is calling on all sweets producers across the British Isles to send in sweets, namely chocolates and butterscotch, en masse. Major producers Cadbury and Callard & Bowser were initially contracted to do the work, but due to the immense volume of sweets required, the Princess is now requesting the help of independent sweets producers. Your place of business will receive payment in the following weeks to produce two thousand butterscotch candies by December 10th, 1914. Please bring the product to regional shipping centers with the appropriate forms filled out. Regional shipping centers are listed on the attached page.

The letter continued, but the words swam.

Two thousand! I whistled.

"What have I told you about eating the bonbons, Jim? They're for customers."

She didn't sound angry this time—just tired. I turned to see Mum in the doorway, shrugging off her coat. I hadn't notice it last night, but it was obvious now that she'd lost quite a bit of weight.

"Looks like you got a big order." I held the letter up. "Why don't you read your mail?"

"I read the mail," she snapped, "just not that letter. I must have forgotten it."

Maybe that was true, but there was still a whole pile of unopened letters. I decided not to ask any more about it, afraid it would set her off.

"So, I've been trying to get a job," I said. I hadn't really tried at all yet, but still. I was planning to start any moment.

"Oh?"

"Maybe as the paper boy or something. There's so many jobs out there, you know."

"Hmm."

She didn't care.

"I've decided I should give half the money to you. You know, since I owe you and all."

She gave a single, high pitched *ha*. "I don't need your money. I have my own business. I'm doing just fine."

"What can I do for you, Mum? How can I help?"

She tilted her head, as if suddenly realizing I was serious. She headed toward the shop, paused in the doorway, and turned around to look at me. "Bring Luther back."

"You want a job as a paperboy?" Mr. Surrey of the Leamington Courier asked, leaning over the counter, wiping the sweat off his forehead with a cloth. He had his sleeves rolled up, forearms dotted with ink from the rushing printing machines.

I put my hands in my pockets and peered around the building. There was a warehouse in the back with all of the printing machines and then a few offices for the journalists and administrators clicking away on their typewriters.

"Yeah, I think so. Paperboy sounds nice."

"You're not a boy, though. How old are you—twenty-five, twenty-six?"

"Twenty-four."

Mr. Surrey chuckled, shaking his head.

"If you're that desperate for a job, why don't you just join the army? You know they've set up a recruiting office in old Carraway's Pub."

"Eh, I don't know."

"Okay, then the navy, the engineers, the munitions factories."

"I did work for a munitions factory, actually. But they let me go. We had some disagreements."

Mr. Surrey stopped laughing, tilting his head.

"Wait a second, I know you from somewhere. You're someone's kid—the sweet shop. Why don't you work there, with your Mum?"

"We've had disagreements, too."

"I could see that. Working with family can be tricky. Well, sorry," he shrugged. "We don't have anything for you here."

"So we have a disagreement?"

Mr. Surrey frowned. "What? No. No disagreement. I'm just not hiring another paperboy. Especially a 24-year-old one. So best be on your way." He turned away and that was that.

By noon, I was hungry, but only had a few folded-up pound notes in my pocket—a couple days' worth of meals. If I wanted to stretch it out, I'd eat breakfasts and dinners at Lavinia's and spend money on outside meals only when necessary. So I didn't eat lunch and instead took a smoke sitting on the curb next to the church. Much more economic. And good for the lungs. I'd been sitting there a few minutes, replaying the conversation with Mum in my head. *Bring Luther back?* I wished I had a decent comeback. *What—you want me to slip across the Channel, evade all the U-boats, find Luther's regiment, and somehow just bring him back home. Sounds easy enough.*

The businessmen in bowler hats strolled down the cobblestone, and an automobile grumbled by, spewing smoke. A flutter, and a little robin landed a few feet off, hopping from brick to brick, picking up pieces of straw in its beak. I remained steady so as not to scare it.

Click. A silver ten pence landed on the pavement, the noise scaring away the bird. I realized one of the passersby had thrown the coin to me. Did I look like a beggar? I definitely hadn't shaved in a month, and my pants were threadbare at the knee, but I was no beggar. Not yet. I swept the coin between the sewer gratings, where it splashed into last night's gurgling rain runoff. I stood up.

"Excuse me, sir."

There were two girls, around the same age as me, dressed in all black—hats, lace, gloves, handbags.

"What do you want?"

"Enlist for your country, coward," one handed me a white feather. The other girl nodded behind her.

I flashed them a grin.

"I'll wear it as a badge of honor."

I tucked the feather in my chest pocket. They turned their chins up at me and marched down the street. Once they'd disappeared around the corner, I quickly left because people were staring. I headed past the church, under the train bridge where it was dark and damp amidst the rubbish bins. Tearing the white feather out of my chest pocket, I dropped it in the rubbish and touched the glowing end of my cigarette to it. It smoldered, each end glowing orange and then slowly curling up black and crusty. I set the feather atop a crumpled newspaper in the rubbish bin, which flared up in flames. *Uh oh.* Soon, the whole bin would be alight and burning—what was I thinking? I spotted a puddle where the cobblestone sank in. Grabbing the bin in both hands, I dumped the contents—brown apples crawling with maggots, mud-matted twine, wet cardboard, all of it—into the puddle, which gave a puff of steam before going out. I left the scene.

I was passing in front of Doc Abbot's office, collar up, hands in pockets, when I saw a group of four men coming down the road, from lunch at Carraway's Pub, no doubt. They were all well to do—sleek suits, gold chains and pocket watches, paisley satin cravats. Were they lawyers? I turned the other way; one of them had a black eye.

"Oy," Mr. Stoker called, "You there!"

I considered turning into the alley to run but realized I'd be giving myself away.

"Yes?" I turned around. "Do I know you?"

"I knew I'd recognized you," Mr. Stoker said deep and slow. "Jim Baker." He looked me up and down appraisingly. "It's been a long time, Jim. How are you?"

"Unemployed."

A frown flickered across his face. He pulled me aside, putting an arm around my shoulder, and told his lawyer friends he would meet them later.

"Jim," he began, "I watched you grow up alongside Rodney since you were a boy. Now, it's no secret you were quite a rascal then, but it cannot carry on any longer. I say this from concern; the road you're on is obviously leading to a dark place. I'd like to see you become a man—strong, bold, proud. I could help you—"

"What happened to your eye?" I changed the subject.

"Oh, nothing. I was out in the country. Equestrian mishap."

"A horse kicked you in the eye? Wouldn't you be dead? It looks more like someone slugged you."

"Well, I did come across a ruffian in the streets the other night, but I—" he froze in mid-speech.

"Well, I just got here this morning, but I'll be sure to keep an eye out for ruffians."

He gave me a long, considering look. "You're not listening to me. You must aspire to achieve more with your life—greatness, Jim, greatness! Why Rodney is on the Continent right now, and—"

"Alright, I'm done here. Get your arm off me."

"Jim, I know you never had a father figure, but I …"

He kept talking on and on in that mythical, elevated tone about greatness and history and something about Sir Francis Drake. I glanced behind us; the lunch-goers had all returned to work by now, and the street was empty. We were just passing under the shadow of the train bridge, where the pile of rubbish I'd dumped still smelled like smoke.

Grabbing Mr. Stoker by the shoulders, I shoved him hard against the brown brick, and he gave a grunt of struggle. I figured I'd been in more fights in my 24 years than he'd seen his whole sorry life. He was flabby and full of himself, while I was taut and lean and knew my limits. He didn't dare move.

"It was you," he whispered, touching his eye.

"Bring Luther back. You know he's unfit to serve."

"Tell that to a court of law, and they'll bring him back, all right. Back and straight to the asylum for him. We both know what Luther did to Rodney. You're lucky I don't turn you both over to the constable and press charges for assault. Unhand me!"

"I see you've found a new wedding ring. Wonder if Mrs. Stoker knows what happened to the original."

His nostrils flared, and I tightened my grip on him.

"Unhand me, Jim."

I stepped back. "All you had to do was ask nicely."

He brushed his sleeve and straightened his coat. "You know, Jim, there's talk in Parliament of enacting mandatory military conscription by Christmas. Objectors would not be treated kindly. As a distinguished lawyer, I would have more than enough reason to hand in your name."

"Why does everyone want me to fight?"

"Maybe everyone thinks you're a bum."

I scowled. "Maybe I don't care what everyone thinks."

"This is an opportunity, Jim. Think of it. I don't have the power to bring Luther back, but maybe you can ensure his survival. Travel to the front, and save him yourself. Travel to the front, and win the respect of all your peers while building the empire up to greater heights than any of our ancestors could have ever imagined."

I looked at the ground and noticed the puddles jiggling with concentric waves. Soon, the stone bridge started vibrating above us—a train was coming.

"Got a job offer already, so you can just bugger off," I muttered.

"What job?"

"The Royal Engineers, they offered me a position, and I said I'd take it. Delivering Christmas gifts to the troops.

So I don't know what you're talking about when you say I'm a bum."

The train tooted its whistle—faint, but growing louder.

"Well, I—I apologize. You should have said something."

"Just remembered."

With the train passing right over us, the thundering pistons and roaring furnace drowned out my words. The whistle shrieked as I brushed past Mr. Stoker, knocking him against the overturned rubbish bin. He tripped, lost his footing on the slick cobblestones, and slipped onto his arse. His yelp of surprise was drowned out by the train, and I watched as he struggled to his feet. He didn't notice the small packet of letters that dropped out of his coat pocket, but I did. After he left the tunnel in a huff, I picked them up. They were from Rodney.

December 17ᵗʰ, 1912

Mother and Father,

I do point out that this letter may take a while to reach you at home, for my pals tell me the mail from India is inefficient, to say the least. But all matters aside, my days in India are now coming to a close. I have enjoyed them tremendously—I have seen elephants and tigers and thick jungles and have tasted many exotic foods. However, the officers have received orders to return from our colonial duties back to England in light of German aggression, as you have likely read about in the paper. We will be stationed at Shorncliffe Camp for training in the coming months, though beyond that, I cannot say. Perhaps you could come visit while I am there?

Some of my pals are making bets that Britain will go to war any day now, and we are filled with both great excitement and great dread. You remember Bill Moore, right? He's told us all that if war is declared, he'll buy beers for the whole battalion. I would love the chance to prove my mettle and would likely have a good many adventures if we do end up fighting on the continent. I presume the fighting would be a little more intense than we saw in India, but then again, I would be more experienced than any of my opponents.

This is an exciting time to be a young man serving God and King. I pray often that the Lord is pleased with us.

Your loving son,
Rodney

August 4th, 1914
Mother and Father,

And so it begins! I am terribly excited, fortified with courage and feel the strength in my arms. I am ready to fight; I have trained with great success at Shorncliffe. Although our instructors are tough, I know it will be necessary for discipline during the chaos of fighting. Already, our battalion has been summoned ███████

███████████████ *in case of a German sea-to-land invasion, or even a zeppelin raid, God forbid. We leave by* ████████████ *so I hope that you will come visit me at Shorncliffe before I leave again.*

Your loving son,
Rodney

◄●►

August 20th, 1914
Mother and Father

We did not stay long at ██████████ *for the navy has the area staked out pretty well with* ██████████ *whatnot. Right now, I am cramped in with about a hundred other men on the train down to* ██████████ ▬ ████ *where we will join up with some other battalions in the 10th Brigade. We will all join the other brigades for the 4th Division of the Expeditionary Force. It doesn't smell very nice here on this train with all these sweating soldiers, so we have opened the windows to smell the nice countryside.*

I will admit that sometimes I have dreams about combat, and they always end up with me being killed by Germans or whatnot. However, I face these thoughts with courage and a stiff upper lip, as you have taught me, Father. Once we reach ██████████ ██████████████████████ *and help out those poor fellows being chased out of Belgium. I pray to God for a safe passage across the channel, for the thought of the German under-sea boats lurking beneath fills me with*

185

terror. But through the grace of God, the strength of my mind, and my excellent training, I know I stand a better chance than most.

Father, I would let you know that you have had a profound impact on my life and have instilled in me courage and morals of the highest order. Mother, I would let you know that your words bring me comfort and tranquility, even in my greatest terrors. I will see both of you soon, and if all goes well, the war will be over before Christmas.

Your loving son,
Rodney

◆❀◆

August 22nd, 1914
Mother and Father,
My regiment departed from ████████████
████████████████████████ Do not worry, the trip is already over, and it was a success. I am currently safe in ████████████████████████████████ As I write this letter, I am lounging in my camp tent on a farm outside the city. I have a full stomach and am relatively warm, so life is good. During the passage across the channel, not a single under-sea boat harassed us, although several of the men vomited from the sea sickness. I was not among them because I am used to long sea voyages, having sailed to India and back. I hope the two of you are well and receive my letter. It sounds like you did not receive my last letter, so I am currently in the dark.

One thing I have noticed is that there are quite a few brothels in ▮▮▮▮▮ *Many of my pals—I will not say who—frequent them and often invite me to come along. That is the reality, but I refuse them and instead stay at the camp. That is, in fact, why I'm alone at the camp now. I recall, Mother, what you said to me before I departed, and I assure you I have never stepped foot inside a brothel. Father, I hope I have lived up to your example of decency and maintained my honor.*

> *Your loving son,*
> *Rodney*

◆●◆

August 27ᵗʰ, 1914
Mother and Father,

Just a few days ago, we had a run in near a little town called ▮▮▮▮▮ *(or something like that, I don't know how the French spell it). Once again, don't worry. I got off with quite a few bruises and a bullet brushed my leg, but I'm able to carry on just fine. I can't speak of the battle in detail; I will only say that* ▮▮▮▮▮▮▮▮▮▮▮▮▮▮▮ *Once again, don't worry. I got off with quite a few bruises and a bullet brushed my leg, but I'm able to carry on just fine. I can't speak of the battle in detail; I will only say that.*

Even that sounds like too much detail. Neither of you could understand what true combat is like, and it sounds so out of place for the words to be spoken with

187

home and my old life in mind. So that is all I will say of the imagery. Do not ask me about it.

We were ordered to march out with all our wagons to set up a defensive line out in a field, but the Germans were also on the move with too many numbers. We were ordered to retreat, but by the time we reached a little town called (I think) ███████ command changed orders again, telling us to dig in and fight, which made everyone a little flustered because we hadn't set up the artillery in time and were being fired at. The only option was to entrench ourselves. So we dug like mad until we had linked enough foxholes together to run the entire length of the ridge. The trenches are an odd sort of place. ████████████████████████████

████████████████████████████

████████████████████████████

███████████████████████ Some of the other divisions were manning lines at other nearby villages, all of them along the ridge. Most of the fighting happened ████

████████████████████████████

███████████████████████ so luckily, we took the left-over end of the fighting. They say we knocked up the Huns pretty well, but it didn't seem that way to me. When the sun set, we retreated and didn't stop our march until after it was dark and we reached the town of ███████ where I am currently camped now and am writing this letter. I was terribly exhausted and had gone several days without sleeping. My eyes closed while I was marching, and for the first time, I experienced what they call "sleeping on your feet."

But I repeat that I am well, and you should not worry for me. I hope everything is going well in Leamington.

Your loving son,
Rodney

CHRISTMAS EVE, 1914
THE WESTERN FRONT

~ LUTHER BAKER ~

I said goodbye to the good German in the pointy hat and he said Merry Christmas to me and I carried Rodney over the mud and the tree trunks and the wires and the bodies and when we got close to the trench they yelled because they thought I was German and I yelled back and said its me Luther Baker and Rodney Stoker is hurt bad and they said hurry and I went into the British trench and everyone yelled and asked me questions they thought everyone was dead and then they took Rodney Stoker away and I didn't see him anymore. The man with the big hat came out and said I was going to get a metal, but I told him I didn't want any metal because it hurts but he said nonsense that I was a hero and I deserved a metal and he was going to see to it that I got what I deserved and so I said thank you. He shook my hand and slapped my back and seemed nice and so I told him the Germans spoke to me and gave me a paper with writing on it and said they don't want to shoot anyone on Christmas. I showed the paper to the man and he tore it to shreds.

Then the man talked to everyone some more and said we are going to attack the Germans because they won't know about it and we might not come back alive and he said we will leave on Christmas morning. He said we all needed to be brave like me because there were people back home who needed us to save them. I asked how many days until Christmas and they said tomorrow is Christmas and everyone is going to attack the Germans on Christmas to try and get inside Germany. One of the pals called the man in the hat a bastard and said no way I am tired of fighting and the Germans are too just look at Luther's note and the man in the hat took that man away and we didn't see him anymore. Someone gave me some food and everyone grumbled and stomped and sang angry songs around the fire. After I ate, I went into the concrete room to sleep and it was filled with water because of the rain that came through the ground. I sat in the corner and could not think and could not sleep and I did not want to be in the world. I just wanted to be home with Mum.

I stayed in the world because I had to give Mum the letter Rodney Stoker wrote for me to tell her I was okay so she would not worry and so she would not be sad anymore.

SEPTEMBER, 1914
THE WESTERN FRONT

~ MESSINES RIDGE ~

For a thousand years, scribes wrote of the Belgian hamlets. There was Ypres in the North, a skeleton of concrete and stone and all things that would not burn. From there, the River Lys curved like a trail of saliva, parting cratered fields in two, where soldiers on each side buzzed and bled. The infested copses and crossroads all along the river, through Hollebecke and Messines and Ploegsteert, all the way to Ypres's twin skeleton, Armentieres.

Radiating from the river, the land gave way to a muddy stew of sandbags, barbed wire, and bloated bodies. And east of the river, in the highlands eroded by runoff streams, soldiers wearing pointed *Picklehauben* huddled together to rub their hands for warmth. Occasionally, one would stand tall to stretch the weariness out of his arms. A crack of some distant sniper, and his comrades would watch his finger splash into the mud at their feet. He'd take his time sauntering for the hospital tent, stopping by the mess tent to stuff some bread and sausage inside his helmet. With any luck, he'd land a week in the hospital and never have to fight again. Later, the rats caught the scent of his fallen finger, and they converged into a writhing, squirming mess. The rats would end up pinned to the bunkers from their tails.

Down the slopes, across the river, the British wallowed in the lowlands, where the water table rose up knee-high through the mud. One of the infantrymen paused, his boot stuck in it. He pulled, but it did not budge. He called for his pals, who finally dragged his foot out, but without the boot. They looked down at his bare foot, pruned and peeling, and shrugged.

Soldiers were always shoveling, digging runoff trenches to channel the chalk-water into the river. No amount of dams or canals could divert the water because it seeped up from below. Some of the trenches eroded so much that they were no longer trenches, but little gullies in which soldiers waded, hiding from the German guns. Even then, the trenches eroded, and soon they weren't tall enough to conceal anything. So the men filled sandbags with forty pounds of mud and stacked them high, dodging sniper fire each time they slung one up on higher ground.

Soldiers passed the nights huddled around glowing cigarette butts. Anyone who lit their smoke too close to the frontline would soon drop it in the mud and fall to their knees, along with half their brains. Smokers and non-smokers alike breathed plumes of steam from their nostrils and pulled their arms close to conserve heat. Their boots were filled with water, their coats saturated, their undergarments half frozen. When rain *taptaptapped* along the trenches, the soldiers shivered with fever and could not keep food down or grab even a few moments of shut-eye. They walked the trenches lightheaded, half asleep, scratching at their lice.

Further out, telegraph wires crisscrossed the reserve trenches, behind which commissaries boiled turnips and artillery nozzles blasted shells into No Man's Land.

Some trenches faded to a lucky hedgerow that still grew between stray craters and the ruins of bombed-out barns. These followed the roads down to farmsteads where weeds grew thick on fallow fields. And along that road lived a regiment of beggars and prostitutes, once mothers and fathers and sisters, who had not even their dignity to sell for a franc. They clung onto the arms of any soldier they saw, shouting in Dutch and French and English and Walloon. Occasionally, soldiers would throw them bread.

Most families had left their farms earlier that summer. Packing all their belongings onto wagons, they locked, for the last time, houses that took generations to build. But some remained because they had nowhere to go. They stayed and housed soldiers, asking them for what they desired most, offering it at twice the price—turnips, chickens, cows—only to find their horses the next morning, laying in the road, stripped bare. Some of the barns became army headquarters, and officers would lay out maps and help the engineers set up telegraph wires.

Nearby, soldiers that sat in the prairies near their billets would shit en masse on little wooden toilets in the fields. They watched the robins. It was pleasant, peaceful even. Afterwards, they would walk down the road to the village brothels—Ploegsteert, Romarin, Messines—

raiding homesteads for alcohol along the way. In abandoned cellars, they often found bottles of wine which they would drink while off-duty, laughing and weeping, because any emotion was better than reality. During their strolls, officers would find them drunk or passed out and sentence them to a few days in jail.

Duty would call, and the soldiers left their billets when the sun rose. They did not sleep those nights, and in the quiet moments, they would look up at the stars where once they saw God and now saw nothing. Philosophy, government, money, family—what did any of it matter when the most enlightened nations led by the most enlightened kings could not prevent *this*? The sons of teachers or gardeners or farmers would be soldiers forever, bound to crawl and charge and shoot on command.

One afternoon, the hazy outline of a man in khaki broke over the horizon. Then came another, and another behind him. Hundreds, then thousands, then tens of thousands filled the trenches shoulder to shoulder, ten men deep. Reinforcements. The men began to whisper to each other when the commissary handed out higher quality meats and when they saw the faint outline of artillery rising along the German trenches. They knew the bubble was swelling.

Daily shelling rounds lengthened, and soldiers crowded into their concrete-enforced bunkers for two days at a time. For two days, they paced from the bedpost to the wall and back with the full knowledge that their bunker could be hit at any moment. At first, the men were steely cool, but as the hours wore on, they flinched and jumped every time the ground rumbled and the lights flickered. At night, flares lit up the world like lightning so the aeroplanes could see. They ate rats because they could not leave the bunker. A few tore their hair and ran outside, into the open. Nobody saw them after that, and the rations were bigger because of it. As the sun rose on the second day, and the sky turned red, the ground stopped rumbling, and the soldiers' eyes met, knowing what would come next. In the pale hours, they smoked their cigarettes and nodded to their pals.

"If you meet your sticky end out there, can I have your coat?"

"Take what you like."

"I keep a secret stash of cigarettes in my trousers. You'll have to fish it out if my body is still intact."

"Cheers, mate."

They would pat each other on the back, swallowing down their terror while others would seclude themselves and pray feverishly. "If you spare me, Lord, I will dedicate my life to you," they'd say through tears.

Some were too afraid to pray. They hid in bunkers, where they raved like cornered dogs at anyone who tried to move them. Officers would have to force them into battle at gunpoint.

Some, with shaking hands, scrawled notes to wives or childhood sweethearts or mothers and fathers, often unable to finish because the horn would sound and commanders would call the charge. A line of men nine miles wide and ten bodies deep climbed ladders and threw themselves into the fray as the German line flashed with gunfire and artillery smoke hung in the air like morning fog.

The first line of soldiers stepped on the mines. Craters spat out plumes of black earth tall as a cathedral's spire and so thick that debris from one explosion could not land before the next explosion went off. Then the second line of men dove for cover inside the craters. Some craters were so slick and steep-sided that soldiers clawed at the edges until the strength left their arms, and they slipped down into the muck.

Survivors called out that the Germans were reloading, and men crept from crater to crater, drawing closer each time. Soon, they approached the barbed wire, which snagged on their clothes so that the more they kicked, the more entangled they became, and the easier they were for the Germans to target. But still more soldiers came, more than the Germans had ammunition for.

When enemies came face to face, all human reason dissolved. Everything became a weapon—mud was for blinding, hands were for tearing, rocks were for throwing. Occasionally the British established little colonies in the enemy trenches, all the way down to the shore of the river, just below the ridge. By the time pale hours of morning changed to dawn, and dawn to high noon, the lines had not moved.

In the shadows at each end of the trenches, near Ypres and Armentieres, mounted cavalries trotted with binoculars and notebooks, writing down what they saw. Pinned down by gunfire, they camped on the spot for several days, observing battle lines ebb and flow with the phases of the moon. A regiment of khakied men, dark-skinned and wearing turbans—the Indian regiments—came to their aid. They rode back to headquarters, where officers convened to frown at maps and scratch their heads. After hours of deliberation, they realized the time for clever battle strategy had ended, and they had only one choice left.

"Send in more troops."

Noon turned to evening, which became dusk, and on the roads leading in and out of the Flemish countryside, never-ending lines of men with one arm, no arms, one leg, or any other possible arrangement of limbs limped through the darkness toward battlefield hospitals in abandoned churches where doctors offered each soldier a blanket. On the other side of the road, ranks of fresh soldiers marched in twos, headed for the front, holding their guns close.

By the third day, the German shells became more spaced out, and their reinforcements scrawnier. Then, the reinforcements stopped altogether. The khakis poked their heads out of their trenches, hearing the lack of gunfire. For the next two days, they inched forward, crouched low, bayonets pointed. Each trench they uncovered lay abandoned, each of the ruined villages empty. They raided the German commissaries for sausage and bread, tearing into them to ease their hunger. They crossed the river on a pontoon bridge the engineers had thrown together. All the while, the Germans watched from afar.

For ten days, the two brigades lived a field away from each other, each knowing that the next offensive would be their last; there simply weren't enough reinforcements left. The men, who hadn't slept in four days, took turns manning the guns so they could at last get some shut eye.

"How about a fire?" one man asked as he shivered under a wool blanket. Along with some of his mates, he sat amidst ammunition crates that elevated them from the water and blocked out the icy wind.

"Forget the fire," another man said. "The Huns will see. I'd light a cigarette, but I don't have any left."

"Here, have one of mine."

"I'll trade you for it. What do you want?"

"Nothing. I'm passing 'em around."

"That's awful decent of you."

The soldier took the cigarette, lit it, and passed it to the right. Each man inhaled one puff of warmth to bring feeling back to their lips and then passed it to the right again. "I wish I could see my wife right now," one said.

"Hmm."

"You have a sweetheart, Rodney?"

"In my mind. Not theirs."

A few chuckles. "Who? Your mum? Come on, now."

"I don't talk about women in that way," was all he said.

They quieted down as a clean uniform walked by. This man wore gloves and a loop around his shoulder: Captain Blanding. He glared down at them and Rodney, along with a few others, leapt up and snapped a rigid salute. One man, huddled further down the trench—a bearded man with mud smeared on his face and with bags under the bags under his eyes—stayed curled up on ground, speaking to no one. Looking at no one.

Captain Blanding passed Rodney's group and stood over the silent man. The man didn't look up. The officer pulled off his gloves. No movement. "Soldier!"

No movement. "Soldier! Do you hear me?"

"Maybe he's dead," someone whispered.

"Blasted infantrymen!" the captain huffed. "I'd write you up if I weren't in such a hurry." He turned back to address Rodney's group and others down the line. "We're expecting a dozen new machine guns tomorrow along with reinforcements. You two," he pointed at two minding their own business, "come with me to stake out nests for the machine guns. The shelling will begin again at dawn, so the rest of you better be ready."

The two designated soldiers sighed and left the warmth of the circle after Captain Blanding. They would spend the next eight hours of darkness shoveling, hammering in posts, laying wire, and heaving forty-pound sandbags into place. Then, when dawn came, they would haul in the new guns and crates of ammunition and spend the rest of the following day picking off Germans who had their backs turned. Those who remained in the circle continued passing the cigarette until it burned out.

"These officers can burn in hell."

"Don't talk that way."

"Why, what are they going to do? Punish me? It's just, so—*God.*"

"Look! The silent one is alive after all," someone said.

Rodney turned and saw the bearded man with mud on his face. He'd uncurled himself and was now on his knees with his hands in the mud.

"Hey you," Rodney called. "Why didn't you salute earlier? Better watch the captain. He has a temper."

No response.

"Hello? What's your name?"

No response.

Rodney pulled himself to his feet and sloshed through the mud until he squatted down beside the man. "Hey, you okay?"

No response.

Rodney reached out and pulled the man's dangling dog tags out so he could read them. He dropped the dogtags with a gasp.

❧

Mother and Father,

I have been fighting for three straight weeks now without much rest. We managed to ███████████ ███████ *chase the Germans back, and now* █████████ ███ *I have trudged through water and mud for many days. I am well. I hope you are well. William Moore and Stephen Wilkins got caught in the open. Their parents will need to be comforted back at home.*

Even though I had experience in India, I was terrified at first by the fighting, but now it does not bother me. If they call for shelling, my body jumps for cover of its own accord. I have become part animal. The new instincts I have gained have helped me more than any amount of training. Combat passes quickly, like a bad dream. Even if the combat lasts for several days or even weeks, without sleep, I still feel like only a day has passed, and my stomach becomes hungry for supper. I feel like I am ice skating over the top of life and watching it from the above. By the time I get a chance for rest in the billets, my feelings come back to me and I realize how barren and unfeeling and indifferent I have become. I am resigned in the face of fate. I will do what I can, but when my time comes, there will be nothing anyone can do. You must be ready for this.

The younger recruits do not understand this. They are terrified and are wide-eyed. Some of them hide in the bunker with locked joints, and nobody can persuade them to move. Others, led by fear, charge wildly and are ▮▮▮▮▮▮▮▮▮▮▮▮▮▮▮ I have tried to help some of them, and it is rather pitiful. It is not uncommon for them to lose control of their bowels during combat.

▮▮▮▮▮▮▮▮▮▮▮▮▮▮▮▮▮▮▮▮▮▮▮▮▮▮▮▮

▮▮▮▮▮▮▮▮▮

Countless other things have happened as well.

I am well and strong. Do not worry.

Rod

P.S. Do you know how to get rid of lice? I now understand where the word "lousy" comes from.

P.P.S. The officers say another battle will begin any day now. By the time you receive this letter, I will probably be deep in combat.

~ RODNEY STOKER ~

For a moment, I fancied myself back in Leamington on that Easter day when I was a boy and saw Luther standing over me in that old lady's garden, his chubby, expressionless face shadowed by the sun. I shivered and touched the back of my head, where I felt that scar through my hair. All the dreams came back, all the blokes I'd fought until I felt that high point where I wasn't afraid anymore. Yes, I was afraid ... of Luther. Or should I say, *I* wasn't afraid, but my *body* was. It was a tricky thing, really. I didn't know why, but when I was a boy and saw him walking down the street, I'd flinch. Now, here I was, a grown man, a soldier, and I couldn't escape him.

Luther stuck out his hand, and I drew back. He was offering me a little ball of mud.

"Thanks, mate."

It was soft and malleable, and for some reason, I felt the need to maintain that shape and not squish it by accident.

"I don't suppose you remember me?" He didn't answer; he didn't even look up at me. "Luther?"

"Why do you know my name?"

"I used to be your neighbor."

"No you didn't."

"Yeah, my name's Rodney Stoker. I used to play with Jim all the time."

"I don't remember you."

"You gave me a nasty scar when you were nine, remember?"

"Mum told me not to talk about that."

"But you know what I'm talking about, though?"

"Everyone here stinks," he said, and he dropped another ball of mud in my palm as if we had previously agreed on it.

I glanced back at the others, who were now trying to find someplace comfortable to sleep. They didn't care enough about the man in the mud to inquire further. Luther would probably die during tomorrow's assault, anyway. They had their own lives to worry about.

"So, how much have you seen?" I asked.

No response.

"Luther?"

"Hmm."

"How much have you seen?"

"You're not talking clearly."

"What?" I said.

"What do you mean what have I seen?"

"The fighting. Done much of it?"

"Just got here yesterday."

Yesterday? But we'd been fighting here since September. He must've come as a reinforcement or something after we crossed the river. I wondered how long he'd been at the front.

"Who are we fighting?" he asked.

"What?"

"Who are we fighting?"

"Germany, who else? Why, how could you not … what kind of question—"

"I have to pee. Where's the loo?"

What the hell? I mouthed to Gordon, who was grinning at me from across the circle.

"We have a latrine a ways back, but it's putrid. Just go find an empty section of trench to pee in, where you won't bother anyone."

Luther nodded and stood up. He was a big man now, taller than the trench.

"*Oye!*" I dove for Luther's legs. We splashed in the bilge, and the crack of sniper fire sent a shower of splinters flying above our heads. One of the officers called out from afar. "Mind your heads over there!"

"Good God," I shook my head at Luther.

He had curled into a ball, his hands clasped over his ears, shaking all over.

"Luther?"

I touched his shoulder, but he didn't react. He just kept rocking. My pals gathered around and looked down at him. They had no room for jokes; they all knew he didn't stand a chance out here. "It's just damn sick they'll let someone like this into the army," my pal Tom muttered. "Damn sick." The others nodded but didn't say anything. I thought that they were being a bit hard on the government.

After the sniper fire, we thought it was a good idea to move to a different part of the trench, so my pals and I migrated down the way and found a cave someone had dug in the mud, where we all gathered into and tried grabbing some sleep. I tried to get Luther to come with us, but he refused. I don't know where he passed the rest the night.

Soon, the pale hours crept back, and the cycle started all over again. Day eleven of living in a trench where I could touch both walls whenever I stretched out my arms. I wondered if I would ever be able to walk in an open field without thinking some sniper was watching me. I finally knew what all those veterans who used to sit in the shade down by the river and reminisce about wars long past were talking about.

When the sun broke over the German artillery, the daily shelling began, and we retreated to the concrete pillbox that had once belonged to the Germans who'd built the trench we now occupied. It was the usual routine. The ground shook, dust fell, and the light bulb flickered out. When the war first started, it made me queasy that I could be blown out of my boots at any moment, but after three months, I'd accepted that there wasn't anything I could do about it. It was a daily part of life.

We heard a knocking on the door.

Tom went to open it, and there was Captain Blanding, holding a pair of binoculars in his gloved hands.

"Good morning, neighbor," Tom said. "Need to borrow some flour?"

"It's been cancelled, Private Wright," he said. "New orders. We're needed down in Plugstreet. Prepare to leave. And you're sentenced to two days in jail once we get there."

Tom smiled.

"Don't get too excited, Wright," Blanding said. "There's a big offensive planned for us next week. Plugstreet will be a battle, alright."

Just like that, we put our hands in our pockets and marched back down the ridge, across the pontoon bridge sitting on the river, back to where we started in early October. But before we said goodbye to our trench, I looked for Luther, but couldn't find him. There was nothing I could do about that, so I trudged toward Plugstreet with the rest of the unit.

For once, it wasn't raining. Given, the mud was still a few inches deep, and our part of the trench had flooded around lunch time. The engineers finally decided to mark the "dam" as a lost cause. Yes, a dam. They'd scrounged a few meters of board from some of the abandoned barns, lashed them together with wire, and painted the seams with tar. They jammed the resulting wall in the River Avon, our name for the ditch next to the machine-gun post the boys called Stratford. It didn't work. I don't know how, but the water just seeped through, around, underneath, whatever which way. As if the dam was a sieve made of cheesecloth.

Eventually, the boards became so soft and saturated that Tom used them for bait in the elaborate mousetrap he'd been working on. That one actually did work—but I don't think because of Tom's genius. So many rats lived in the trenches, getting fat off of us when we weren't looking, that you could close your eyes and shoot and you'd have got one. They'd swim around in the ankle-deep water with chunks of I-didn't-know-what in tow—I hoped it was food, but I didn't want to make any assumptions, so I just tried not to imagine. All of my pals were of the same opinion, and we'd take joy in engineering marvelous ways to hunt the rats. Once, Tom used his own hand as bait. He played dead and lay in the corner until dark, when the rats came out for their nibble. Then, we all jumped out and used the boards of our "dam" to pen them in. They had it coming, the bastards.

We passed the rest of the night in shifts; Tom manned the gun for the first shift while I got some shut-eye. I must've gotten a few hours in, surprisingly, because when Tom nudged my shoulder and I looked up, the sky was full of stars. Breathing out steam and cracking my knuckles, I stepped over the River Avon and into the gun nest. It was a little fortress of shot-up sandbags tucked between two mounds of dirt. It smelled like tobacco and rotten food, only it wasn't food that was rotting. Two other fellows—Appleby and Wallace—met up with me, and we set up the nest for our shift without speaking. Appleby pulled out his binoculars from the box, and Wallace grabbed the ammo. Together, we all leaned on our bellies in the mud and squinted through the dark at the opposing trench.

"See anything, Appleby?" I asked.

I looked at him, and his mustache wiggled up and down.

"Louder, I can't hear you."

His mustache wiggled again; all I could hear was a ringing in my ears. *Aaaah, damn explosions—I'll be deaf before this war is over.* I pointed at my ear, and he handed me the binoculars, and said so I could hear him. "Just a couple Germans walking around."

The grey light of the moon and some lit cigarettes were all I had to see by, but I was able to make out the German line. I saw the pointed tips of their helmets hobbling past the sandbags, up and down, up and down.

Some shrill noise sounded, and we all ducked for cover, breathing fast. The noise sounded again.

Wallace chuckled.

"Just a bird. Shells don't scare us, but birds do."

I was willing to argue that point, but I said nothing and returned to the binoculars.

Germans marched in the two circles of the magnifying lenses. I turned my head and shivered to see another machine-gun post, almost identical to ours. A gunner sat in it—I couldn't make out his face, just his figure—staring right back at us through his binoculars. There were two others with him. Like looking in a mirror. I told the others.

"Should we shoot at them?" Wallace whispered.

Appleby and I shook our heads. "Nah," Appleby yawned, "I don't really feel like it. They'll just shoot back, and we'd be dead before dawn."

"But he's looking right at us," Wallace whispered. "He could kill us at any moment."

"He won't, trust me. He's just as tired of this as we are."

"What about your duty to Britain?"

Then, Appleby told Wallace to piss off. Only, he didn't say piss. I frowned, thinking that was a rather unpatriotic thing to say. But I didn't argue; we were all tired to the point where we said whatever we felt.

Towards the end of the night, a little feather of blue seeped into the sky, just above the German guns. Behind us, privates slowly started filing out of their dugouts, awakened by officers. They filed into the trenches, where they all pulled out their guns and screwed on the bayonets. We were anticipating a German offensive this morning, the one that had been postponed a few weeks prior. It was easier to defend than to attack, and I think most people had figured that out by now. From the nest, I had a nice view of the whole spectacle. I saw the boys writing letters, shaking, sniffling, and praying as they usually did before going over the edge. I caught sight of Tom, who pulled a flask out of his coat—I didn't know how he snuck it in there—and took a swig, which made me frown. I saw Luther, too. He sat alone, trying to lay low I supposed.

Crack! Somewhere out there, a German had pulled the trigger on his *Mauser*, and the sound echoed over the cratered, frosted turnip farm between us.

"Man down! Medic!" someone called.

They rushed a man off on a stretcher, down to auxiliary trenches, where an ambulance would be waiting to take him to the hospital in Hazebrouck.

"Was that Tom?" Appleby clutched his helmet.

We all squinted but couldn't tell because the man was too far away by then.

"I saw him drinking earlier," I said after he disappeared. "Suppose he was preparing himself?"

"Wouldn't surprise me," Wallace muttered, "Tom's a coward."

"One more word, Wallace, I swear." Appleby was red in the face.

Him and Tom had been best pals when they were boys in Warwick. I patted Appleby on the back. "This isn't the time to think about that, Appleby," I said, "or else we'll all end up like Tom."

"'Course." He gave me a fake smile, and we returned our focus to the German line, hands on the gun.

I half expected one of our boys to fire back after that shot, which would've escalated into a little skirmish, a not-quite battle leaving ten or twelve us dead. But nobody fired back this time.

"Stoker, Wallace, Appleby!"

We all jumped to see Blanding behind us.

"You just let one of our boys get shot. Retaliate, or the Huns will walk all over us."

Appleby opened his mouth to say something but then closed it.

"Yes, sir," I said, training my eyes on the machine gun with the officer breathing down my neck.

I looked down the sight to see the little pointed helmets moving up and down with the Germans' breathing. I coughed awkwardly, grabbed the two handles and nudged the gun, so gently that Captain Blanding wouldn't notice.

Aiming at the dirt just in front of the trench, I pulled the trigger. The gun burst to life, the muzzle flashing white like a firecracker as the ammunition fed into it, the little cartridges clinking to the ground while the smoke curled off in ribbons. The gun rattled with every shot, several times a second, and I felt the vibration in my bones. We did a bang-up job shooting that dirt, and by the time the gun overheated, we'd left probably a hundred, two hundred bullets lying in the field. We'd probably riddled a couple unlucky turnips, but that was it. Blanding had already moved on. Across No Man's Land, I heard the Germans call out to each other in surprise, while down in our own trench, the infantrymen prepared for the defensive, each of them set up at their posts. Suddenly, the ground in front of us lit up, and Wallace swore. All three of us ducked low behind the sandbags, but soon we realized that the Germans were only shooting at the dirt, just as we had.

"Do your worst!" one of the Germans shouted at us.

Wait a second.

"They speak English?" I asked nobody in particular.

"'Course they do. Half of 'em are our Saxon cousins," Appleby muttered. "Some likely lived in England before the war. My own Uncle Gabriel is German. Moved to London to work as a waiter, was called back by the Kaiser when the war started."

"So they're half British."

Appleby wiped his nose, "More or less."

"Then why are we even fighting them?"

Suddenly, a few more guns went off; more Germans were firing at the dirt. Our boys answered back in a like manner, and soon we'd fired so many bullets into the dirt that giant brown clouds hung stagnant under the sunrise.

"What is this?" Wallace threw his binoculars at the ground. "A fake battle? Where's the discipline?"

I was rather uneasy with the whole situation, knowing I'd directly disobeyed Captain Blanding. Thought there might be some punishment. After all, not fighting the enemy was the same as fraternizing with the enemy. And that was punishable by court martial.

We kept up our work of firing at the dirt until noon, when finally, someone came to relieve us. The first thing I did after was find a quiet corner of the trench and piss. I buttoned my pants back up, slung my rifle over my shoulder, and sloshed through the chalky water over to the rest of the boys. I set up at an empty spot in the line and took aim at a little messenger pigeon fluttering over German heads. I missed. *Damn.* The sun started to sink again, and the German offensive we'd been warned about never came. Odd.

"Captain Blanding got a telegraph from further up the line, said the Germans chose to attack at Ypres instead," the boy at my right filled me in.

"Well, that's nice. So we can just keep this up until dark and then head over to billets?"

"Looks that way."

The boy aimed high and shot down one of the pigeons. Across the turnip field, we heard clapping, and German voices going, "Yaa, yaa."

"Ooh, Good shot! You got a round of applause out of them," I turned to him. "Say, what's your name?"

Crack!

The boy crumpled to the ground, my face and the front of my coat spattered with him.

◆

Since we'd lasted until November, the sun set early, which meant darkness fell around supper time. I slopped some veggies and meat into my helmet, slung my rifle over my shoulder again, and spooned it out as we all set out on the road. Our stay on the River Avon had come to an end—at least for now. For the next two weeks, it was our turn to cycle out through the billets and get some rest. Me and my pals all marched in twos down the road as the other battalion marched up it. We nodded at each other as we passed but said nothing. I hoped they'd pull through without too much trouble.

Marching was one of the more preferable activities for a soldier, I'd gathered. It didn't require much thought or risk—although it was guaranteed to leave your feet covered in blisters—and I'd take that any day, judging how things were going. The road passed field after field overgrown with weeds and pocked with crater lakes. A few aeroplanes left exhaust trails in the clouds above us, which caught our attention for a little bit. Dogfights were always interesting to watch, and I wondered what it would be like to be in the air corps. Definitely more chivalrous than being an infantryman, no doubt. I nodded off a few times and then snapped awake to realize I'd carried on sleep walking. We marched just short of eighteen miles—yes,

I'd counted the mile markers on the road signs. Soon, the village of Hazebrouck sizzled on the horizon, miraged by the dawn light reflecting off of the frost. *Thank God.*

Since joining the army, I'd become very good at what I called half-sleeping. Sure, my eyes were closed and drool dripped onto my shirt, but I could still tell you how many men were in the room—particularly, how many of them were armed. It was a sixth sense I'd developed. To prove it, there were thirteen men in the room. Two of them were awake, staring at the ceiling. We'd left our guns leaned together by the door.

Occasionally, my brain would wake me up on its own accord, as if to say, *Watch yourself, Rodney,* and for this reason, I hadn't had a full night's rest in four months. I rolled over onto the hay we stole from the locals, burying myself deep in it to hide from the world. Beams of dusty, white light forced their way in through the cracks in the barn doors, but I only buried myself deeper in the shadow of the hay.

Some of the boys spoke—something about taking a bath and finding a change of clothes. I exhaled comfortably, feeling the gentle pressure of the hay closing off the world around me, and the warmth my body worked all night to stoke up. I was safe. My back ached and my stomach roiled, but nothing could distract me from my sacred work of sleep. In that moment, all was right in my life. I had only several desires. Breathe. Curl up. Adjust legs. Adjust arms. Pull bedding closer. Disappear. Everything else faded to the radio static of jumbled and incoherent directives from my brain's inner drill sergeant.

Youneedtogetupgetwashedgetfoodgogogobeforeitsalltoolatethere'sGermanscominggetupgetwashedgetfoodcleanyourrifleonetwothreefouronetwothreefour...

My forehead throbbed, and I realized I was probably dehydrated. Rolling over, I took a swig out of my canteen and tried going back to sleep. Couldn't. Eventually, I rolled out and creaked open the barn door. I held my hand up against the sun, squinting. In those early minutes after waking up, everything was blinding and fuzzy; when I was a boy, I'd tell my dad there was fire in my eyes. The notion occurred to me that I was still a boy and had no right to look back on my halcyon days with nostalgia. Few of the other men out there had lived full lives already; none of my pals had ever held a job outside of the army.

When boys are young, Dad always said, *they can be molded to fit whatever life adults expect of them—the piano, the gun, the bottle*. Following that logic, I sensed I was nearing the end of my malleable lifespan. The only profession I had ever known was the army. I knew my numbers but never made it past algebra. I could read but didn't know the first thing about Shakespeare. However, I knew to think twice about sticking someone in the ribs because your knife would get stuck and someone else would finish you off first. I knew how to auction off a pack of cigarettes for two pairs of dry socks. I knew how to dodge for cover at the slightest mention of the word *shell*. But I'd never been in love, never held a job, never opened a bank account, never found God. So whenever I got to feeling down during the quiet times that I so feared, I thought to myself that all the other men were going through the same thing and having other humans to struggle alongside can even make Hell worthwhile.

I paced down the road, past the creaking windmill, and through a scattered herd of cows broken out of a pasture. The frost had evaporated a few hours ago; it was about noon, so the grass was hard and cold. Didn't bother me—my only concern was if it was dry or not, and it was, so I walked barefoot, airing out my blisters and letting the grass tickle feeling back into my numb feet. I even took my shirt and coat off and walked around in my suspenders and trousers, just for the sake of some sun. My clothes were ragged, torn, and scraped up, and if an officer saw me, he'd probably write me up for a bad uniform. But the sun on my skin was glorious and worth the risk.

Out in the turnip field, amidst the harvest stubble, I saw a crowd of soldiers naked under a stilted drum of water. They each got a good soaking, rubbing their hands through their hair and washing the mud off their faces. Getting their bath and a clean change of clothes, no doubt. Weren't Wallace and Appleby talking about finding a bath? I approached the men.

"Ah-ah. Officers only, soldier. It's reserved."

God damn. It's like I'm a second-class citizen.

"Yes, sir!" I saluted and turned on my heels.

Across the field, behind some trees, I found another crowd of naked men. They were bathing under improvised showers—coffee cans with holes poked through, which they filled with water out of a central barrel. I spotted Luther amongst them.

"Morning." I walked up behind him while dropping my suspenders and throwing my pants in the pile of dirty clothes.

"It's not morning. It's afternoon."

"Well, then good afternoon."

"No, it's not."

"What?"

"It's not a good afternoon."

Well, pardon me for reaching out. Luther's eyes traveled down to my body. I flinched. "Goddamn, mate, don't you have any boundaries?"

"Are you afraid of me, Rodney Stoker?"

"What the—?" I shook my head at him and quickly walked over to Wallace and Appleby, who were taking weak showers from punctured coffee cans.

"Can I have one of those?"

Wallace handed me his can, which I dunked into the barrel. I drew it out, and the weak little streams of water wetted my hair. Can by can, I washed the smell out of my armpits, the grime off my face and neck, and scrubbed the rest of myself as best I could.

"What's the schedule for today?" I asked Appleby.

He grabbed his uniform from the pile and pulled on his trousers. "First, we find something to eat. After that, we've got drills, shoe shining, medal polishing, a lecture from some officer on STDs. You know, same old."

Although my uniform was still a mess after my bath, I felt clean, and I walked the streets in a state that verged on bliss. What a wonderful morning. I met up with Luther, Wallace, and Appleby at the café, and we each had ourselves a baguette. Appleby said he wasn't hungry and dropped a stick of bread in each our hands. Good man, Appleby. Good man.

About that time, into the café walked a nurse, about my age, with a red cross patched on her apron. Her hair was pulled back tight under a hat. Her wrists and shins were all wrapped tight in white cotton, and I couldn't tell if she was a nun or not, but I felt sick toward the boys who eyed her like she was a piece of meat.

"Luther, I've been looking for you! Thank God you're okay." She reached out to give him a hug, but he backed away from her, eyeing her hands like two swarms of bumblebees.

Luther gave her a curt nod. "Good afternoon, Ethyl Brand."

Ethyl Brand? No wonder she looked familiar!

"I tried to find you before they released you from your evaluation at the hospital, but you'd already gone," Ethyl said. "I am outraged that I can't get anyone to take the doctor's word that you're not fit for the front."

"They made me go back," Luther said. "I didn't like it."

"Luther didn't do any fighting, Miss," Wallace stepped in. "The Huns attacked at Ypres instead, so we kind of just stood there and puttered around for a few days. It was a waste of time, really." Then he stepped closer to Ethyl. "Perhaps you could put in a word to one of the higher-ups that some of our boys are going easy on the enemy."

Ethyl looked at Luther, then to Wallace. "Do you trust this man, Luther?"

"No." He said it without any hesitation.

"What about him?" she pointed to Appleby.

This time Luther hesitated, but then shook his head. "No."

"Is there anyone here you trust?"

Luther knit his brow for two seconds. Then, he pointed at me. "I can always trust that Rodney Stoker will be afraid of me."

"Rodney Stoker?" Ethyl turned and looked at me in surprise. Then she frowned. The frown wasn't a disapproving kind of frown, though, but more a thoughtful kind of frown, like a philosopher thinking deep thoughts. Her jaw clenched, and I could tell she was gritting her teeth, weighing her options. Finally, she nodded, and said, "I have an offer for you. If you're interested, come with me." Ethyl motioned to Luther who stood and followed her out of the café and back down the road toward town. With nothing better to do, I followed after them.

"I've heard it said that the best employee is a fearful one," she announced. "I'm not sure I agree, but I need to know why you fear Luther." The way she spoke, she sounded like a minister or a professor.

"I guess I'm used to people following rules. Luther, he doesn't get rules. He's almost completely outside the rules."

"I almost killed Rodney Stoker when we were kids," Luther said.

Oh boy. I exhaled.

"Rodney Stoker and my brother were fighting, so I pushed Rodney Stoker and he fell on a rock and split his head open and almost died."

"Luther," Ethyl said, "the last time we spoke about this, you said you weren't allowed to talk about it."

"Mum told me never to talk about it, but Rodney Stoker didn't die because he's right here and he knows what happened and my mum isn't here so what does it matter?"

We'd walked back up the road, past the windmill, past the abandoned barn I'd slept in last night. Further up was a cluster of buildings where the roads all met. That was Hazebrouck.

"Rodney," Ethyl turned to me, "how would you like to be home free?"

I nearly choked. "What do you mean home free?"

"I mean, how'd you like to be free from fear, free from fear of Luther?"

"You sure you're not a preacher? Besides, I'm not afraid of Luther."

"Luther thinks you are."

I thought of how every time Luther waved, I flinched.

"Okay," I said, "what of it?"

"I'm a nurse. And if one day you're out on the frontline and take a bullet, and the soldiers rush you to the hospital, there's not much the doctors can do for you. Everyone is usually busy. On a normal day, the hospital is filled well beyond capacity. But what if you just have to say my name, and I'd give you all my attention. How does that sound?"

"It sounds like you only treat patients who do you favors."

She stared at me, like she knew I wasn't done talking. And I wasn't.

"Okay, what's the trade?"

"Cover your ears," she muttered to Luther, and he obeyed like a marionette on a string.

Then she turned to me. "Keep Luther alive."

"That's it? How am I supposed to do that? And what if I fail? Would you really just leave me to die?"

"I might."

"You're raving. Wait a minute, who gave you the authority to put me on Luther duty? What's my commanding officer going to say?"

"Don't worry about that. Will you do it?"

"This is ridiculous. If I see Luther—or any other soldier—in trouble, first thing I'd do is help him out. I don't need bribes."

"First thing you'd do? Really? You wouldn't put your own life first? You see your fellows die every day, and I imagine it means nothing to you. You just pick up their gun and continue shooting. I'm asking you to put Luther's life first. To put your own life on the line if his is at risk."

I stopped and stared at her. "How dare you think I'd do any different? That's what we do for our brothers every damn day! You don't know what I've seen or what I've done or how I feel about any of it. You don't know anything about me!"

I gave a half-rotted fence post at the edge of the road a swift kick and nearly broke my toe, but Ethyl didn't say a word. She just watched me like one of those Greek statues with the empty stone eyes, and right then I wanted to show her what it was like in the trenches, what it was like marching, what it was like in the cold when your feet were frozen and your belly was empty and you've seen your mate blown to bits.

Ethyl did not flinch.

I exhaled and stuck out my hand. "Okay. You've got a deal."

~ ETHYL BRAND ~

To: Mr. Michael Surrey, Leamington Courier
From: Ms. Ethyl Brand

Dear Sir,

Your wonderful publication has done much to enlighten and enthuse me over the years toward the aims of social justice. Motivated by your fine journalists, I have spent my youth seeking meaning in the world, and I think your publication could gain from my vast experiences. For one year, I served as a missionary on the Niger River, where I taught English. I fell ill with malaria and returned to England just last year, where I volunteered with the British Red Cross. In that capacity, I served the wounded soldiers on the Western Front.

I have a unique perspective on world events that you would be hard-pressed to find in most others of my age, and I think my perspective would draw in both female readers and young people seeking the exotic. Currently, I have written several pieces reporting my experiences as both a wartime nurse and a missionary in Africa, although I assume the nursing would be of greater interest to your paper.

I have fair writing skills, considering my work as an English teacher, although you may read for yourself, as I have attached a sample of my work for your consideration.

You may remember me from my youth or be acquainted with my family, as Leamington is the city that raised me. I understand you are in contact with many other publications as well, and I would be appreciative if, should you not find my work to your taste, you would pass this message on to your peers.

Sincerely,
Ms. Ethyl Brand
9 November, 1914

P.S. If you respond during December 1914, please do not mail to the return address, but rather to the Baltic and Corn Exchange Hospital in Calais, France.

Attached: "The Emptiness of the Age"

The Emptiness of the Age
Ethyl Brand

I returned to Europe because I knew what I would find there. The decision to volunteer for the

British Red Cross required little thought. Nay, I would not live with closed eyes, now that they had been opened. I could not.

My first assignment was as a nurse at the Baltic and Corn Exchange Hospital in Calais. After my brief training, the doctors trusted me enough to do the dirty work of cleaning wounds and applying bandages.

One morning, I was hard at work changing the sheets of one of the beds in which a soldier had just bled out. They were scarlet; apparently,

███████████████████████████████████
███████████████████████████████████
███████████████████████████████████
███████████ Regardless, I walked in and changed the sheets. The other men looked at me with fear, some thinking I was a kind of goddess with the power to decide life or death, others with disgust that I could be so uncaring. The truth was, I knew what had happened was a sad thing, but I had seen ████████████████████████████████ In Africa, we would often find tribesmen ███████████

███████████████████████████████████
███████████████████████████████████
███████████████████████████████████
███████████████████████ I taught the native children English and watched them put on suits with their British accents and look with uncomprehending eyes upon their own elders who spoke only in the local tongue.

The soldiers heard this, and I became a sort of prophet to them. They would come to me seeking counsel. One of them asked me if there was a God, and I could not reply. Another asked me if he could be forgiven for all the Germans he had killed. I only said, "Forgive yourself," not knowing what I meant by it, simply led by the notion that it might be of some comfort to him. "What kind of a woman are you?" he asked, and I could tell he wanted me to reply, "A saint. A sage. Something of the like," but I could not.

Soon, the other doctors started coming to me when I was alone, closing the door behind them. They spoke to me of the soldiers they had failed to save and wept in front of me. I listened and laid a strong hand on their shoulder. They asked me what they should do next, to which I replied, "Live," because I thought it sounded comforting. I explained to them that in Africa, the village elders would hold two funerals, the first to mourn a life and the second to celebrate it. Many of the doctors who wept at my feet of a night would not meet my eyes the next morning. Eventually, I learned I had become something of an oracle.

By November, I had heard a sorry tale from just about every person working in the hospital. They began to call me "Mother Brand," and it was fitting, really, because of how the bonnets we wore looked like a nun's habit. Even the nuns sought council from me. I didn't even try to give advice, though, because nothing I knew could ease their pain. I merely listened.

There was a room at the Baltic and Corn Exchange Hospital where men went ███████ None of the soldiers went there willingly; they claw at the walls and call for help as we carted their beds down the hall and the wheels squeaked on the floor. However, often I was the one pushing the cart because none of the other nurses had the strength to. I was the one who stayed with the soldiers to ████████████ praying for them until the light in their eyes finally flickered out. Then, orderlies took the bodies away and I changed the sheets.

As the fighting stagnated in November, and we heard the soldiers had dug themselves in trenches for a long stalemate, the doctors established more permanent hospitals. I remember my superior, a doctor by the name of Mason, soliciting for nurses to train the new volunteers at these clearing hospitals. Dr. Mason came to us in the early morning, while we were all groggy and trying to revive ourselves with coffee. I was ignoring him, concerned only with the poor soldier two floors up suffering terribly from a disease of the reproductive system. The words "Third Corps" and "Fourth Division" crossed Dr. Mason's lips, and I asked him to repeat himself. "One of the clearing hospitals in Hazebrouck is calling for experienced volunteers to serve the wounded of the Third Corps. Would you consider it?" I told him I would for I knew the Royal Warwicks, the boys of

Leamington that I knew fondly, were among the Third Corps.

My peers threw a party for me before I left, and we all gathered in the staff lounge, a tiny hall with a radio, and shared tea and coffee. Due to the rations, there were no sweets of any kind. Ah, sweets. I remembered going to Baker's Sweets on Bath Street as a little girl, whenever I stumbled upon a penny in the gutter. I remembered Ms. Baker and her son fondly. He made truffles like Michelangelo carved marble. Those halcyon days were far behind, though, and I felt a duty to distract people from the fact. After all, to accept it was a death in itself.

I took the train from Calais to St. Omer to Hazebrouck along with three Carmelite nuns. They prayed the rosary through about a dozen times while on the train, but I did not participate even after they invited me. "You are a sister, though, are you not? The doctors call you Mother Brand." I explained to them that it was only a name, only a name. I was proud to be working alongside these women, three veterans who had known intimately every kind of despair a man could face in his final days. As we traveled southeast, the land turned from green to brown. Outside the train window, I saw the occasional crater from stray shells and many boarded-up farmhouses. Blasted tree stumps poked out everywhere, but no forests. Hazebrouck was about twenty miles behind the

British trenches, and if we squinted, we could see the smoke rising over a brown ridge. The whole view could fit behind my thumb, where it would be obscured.

The clearing hospital was spread out amongst a local church, a pub, a barn, a theatre, and many other businesses that had graciously opened their doors to us. I slept at a local convent with the Carmelite nuns and was woken every day at dawn by their eerie Latin chanting, prayers for the healing of the sick. My room was bare and cold except for a crucifix and a skull mounted above my bed. I supposed the skull was a symbol of mortality, which really was fitting for about half of the wounded that came there died. For those men, all I could do was prepare a soft bed. I considered myself a professional pillow-fluffer.

I was only there from November 1st to November 3rd and the wounded we saw arrived by ambulance a little after breakfast. They came from the recent battles out in Flanders. On my second day working there, I could feel the ground vibrate from the shelling at the front, and hear the bombs explode as if they were right outside the door. Stray shells landed in Hazebrouck, destroying several barns, and we soon received orders to temporarily evacuate the wounded.

On the evening of November 9th, I recall having a moment of quiet to myself. It was after my shift, and I was strolling through the village. I looked over the French countryside, and it was really quite pretty.

"Mother Brand!" I heard one of the nurses calling for me, and I was grateful for it. "One of the men is throwing a fit! He's disturbing the soldiers and none of us can calm him."

I threw my cigarette away and followed her to see the commotion. I heard moans echoing down the hall as I entered the foyer. Further down, I saw the figure of a man running about the beds of the soldiers in his underwear. He was banging on walls and knocking over tables, flapping his hands. The man was surely suffering from severe shell shock, but the sight reminded me of a time when I was a little girl and had occasion to witness such behavior in Leamington.

I pulled a dozen pillows off empty beds and threw them into an open space on the ground, where I directed the strong-armed nurses to hold the man down until his attack subsided. He thrashed against them, until finally, his breathing slowed and his lower lip trembled. I read the name on the dog tag and then said to the other doctors, "Leave us. I will take it from here."

This man, whom I will call Smith, was one of my girlhood acquaintances. He was indeed from Leamington, and we had grown from birth alongside each other. I always knew he was born different, and I could not, for the life of me, figure out how he had come to be enlisted. Surely those who cared for him and those who understood his affliction would never have allowed it. With some help, I managed to get him dressed and invited him out on a walk to let the fresh air calm him, but he would not go with me. He would not go out into the open because, he swore to me, a mean man wanted to hurt him. I insisted, but he refused. Finally, I decided to take him to my personal quarters, a nice closed space, where we spoke. Our conversation is as follows.

"Smith, do you remember me? I'm Ethyl Brand. I was friends with your brother. I used to buy your truffles."

"I make the best truffles. The best in the world."

"Can you tell me why you aren't making truffles now?"

"I am."

"What?"

"With mud. I make truffles with mud."

"Chocolate truffles, though. Why aren't you still making those in Leamington, where it's safe?"

He sniffled a little and only said, "He tricked me."

"Who tricked you?"

No answer. Smith grabbed his head and shrieked, and I sat next to him on the bed, hugging him. I noticed the dark circles under his eyes and wondered how long it had been since he'd slept?

"Would you like to take a nap? You can sleep in this bed here."

"Is it safe?"

I nodded. "I've been sleeping here for months, and not one shell has even come close."

"Are you sure?"

"Yes, you're safe here."

"But I have bugs, and I'm dirty."

"I'm bound to get lousy sooner or later."

"Will you stay here, please?"

I nodded and pulled back the covers. He took off his boots, and I saw that his toes were pruned. The rest of his feet were spongy and soft like wet paper, and I was afraid they would tear from all those weeks of walking in filth and freezing water. With a towel, I dried his feet and covered them in lard from my own personal stock, then I told him I would be right back and I took my basin out to the faucet and filled it with water. When I returned, I sponged the dirt off his body and gave him one of my shirts to wear, because at least they were dry. His hair and beard were matted with dirt, so I gave him a good trim and a shave, so short that the lice wouldn't be so much of a bother. While he was under the covers, I tucked in the sheets beneath him so that they hugged his figure like a cocoon. Within moments, he was sound asleep in what I would assume, his first good rest in months. To me, his snores were the music of home, and I curled up on the floor beside the bed and listened to his symphony.

I soon learned that Smith was not wounded, but had only been sent to the hospital with a fever, which he soon overcame. By law, he was required to return to his regiment on the front. Before he left, I made him promise me, "I will not antagonize my officers. I will never be the first to respond to an order. I will not be the first to leave the trench. I will stay in the back of the crowd. I will not leave the sight of the other boys from Leamington, and I will not look over the wall of the trench, no matter how tempted."

When he left in the morning, I marched straight up to the military headquarters, shaking with rage. It was a little cottage just outside of town, sprouting with telegraph wires and antennae. Inside was a radio box and a table plastered with elevation maps. I met with an officer and gave him a good piece of my mind. The officer looked up at me—his chest bedecked in jingling medals, his guns and saber clean and shining and unused—and asked me what in God's name was I going on about. I told him that Smith was unfit to serve, that he had been tricked into enlisting, and that he was breaking the law by keeping him at the front. "Who is Smith? You can't expect me to know all their names," he snarled, and tried shooing me away. But I refused to leave. Finally, he called for an aide and he ushered me out the door by physically picking me up off my feet and setting my outside. Then he bid me Good Day and shut the door in my face.

I approached the general and told him we had a soldier who was mentally unfit and needed to be sent home. The general was in a busy meeting and dismissed me, saying he didn't have time.

If my word wasn't good enough, perhaps the doctors' would be. Afterwards, I went straight to round up a group of doctors and asked them to do an evaluation of Smith. They agreed because they owed me from previous favors. They all collaborated on a letter and strongly recommended Smith be sent home, that a mistake had been made during enlistment. This letter was sent to high command, and they told me to wait a few weeks for a reply.

That is why I am writing this article. This man, Smith, was done a grave injustice and no one cares one whit. I would like to raise awareness for his plight, to let his family know, and to solicit help in any way I can.

Mrs. Ethyl Brand,

By order of the British government, you are commanded to stop writing or face persecution. Effective 8 August, 1914, the Defense of the Realm Act (DORA) outlaws amateur journalism on the Western Front.

Your article has been intercepted and disposed of, and your information will be kept on record should you continue damaging public morale and antagonizing the war effort through your writings.

To: Mr. Michael Surrey, Leamington Courier
From: Ms. Ethyl Brand

Dear Sir,

You may recall that I wrote to you several weeks ago, although the mail, being what it is during wartime, may have not reached you yet. I am, therefore, taking the liberty of writing to you again.

Your wonderful publication has done much to enlighten and enthuse me over the years toward the aims of social justice. Motivated by your fine journalists, I have spent my youth seeking meaning in the world, and I think your publication could gain from my vast experiences. For one year, I served as a missionary in Nigeria, where I taught English to natives and witnessed many evils. I fell ill with malaria, barely surviving, and returned to England just last year, where I volunteered with the British Red Cross. In that capacity, I served the wounded soldiers on the Western Front.

I have a unique perspective on world events that you would be hard-pressed to find in most others of my age, and I think my perspective would draw in both female readers and young people seeking the exotic. Currently, I have written several pieces reporting my experiences as both a wartime nurse and a missionary in Africa, although I assume the nursing would be of greater interest to your paper.

I have fair writing skills, considering my work as an English teacher that I mentioned earlier, although you may read for yourself, as I have attached a sample of my work for your consideration.

You may remember me from my youth or be acquainted with my family, as Leamington is the city that raised me. I understand you are in contact with many other publications as well, and I would be appreciative if, should you not find my work to your taste, you would pass this message on to your peers.

Sincerely,
Ms. Ethyl Brand
4 December, 1914

P.S. If you respond after December 1914, please do not mail to the return address, but rather to the Baltic and Corn Exchange Hospital in Calais, France.

Attached: "Adventures of a Frontline Nurse"

Adventures of a Frontline Nurse
Ethyl Brand

Fate is kind to the soldiers on the Western Front. They are in high spirits and fight with the strength of proud men. I came to serve them as a nurse soon after returning from British West Africa, where I followed my duty to our great nation. But that story is for another time. When I heard the war had finally begun in Europe, I volunteered for the

British Red Cross immediately, if only to serve my God and King.

Upon my arrival in Calais, I quickly learned the normal duties of a nurse. I cleaned the bed sheets and emptied the bed pans—one of the more disgusting and primal duties—but I soon learned it was quite easy work. Whenever I felt like the work was too much, the resilience of these bold soldiers never failed to inspire courage in my bones.

The soldiers were, overall, an admirable group of fellows. They did not blink in the face of despair, but rather ran to the frontlines for every bomb that detonated. I cannot even begin to imagine how many lives they saved each day.

I often heard them singing songs in their hospital beds, and they told me they were quite well and wished they would heal up so they could go back to fight for liberty with their pals. "Take your medicine and we'll see," I told them, and they all laughed. We really did have a good time together.

Soon, I heard word that the hospitals closer to the frontline, particularly out in the village of Hazebrouck, were in need of more nurses. Eager to separate myself from the crowd of volunteers, I took the position along with three nuns, who spoke to me of holy things and kept my morale high. The more time I spent in the hospital, the more I learned how lucky our boys really are to have such skilled nurses. Wounded soldiers enter the hospital by ambulance, babbling about how the Germans were on their last gasp and how the German supply lines had been cut off. In general, they spoke of victory, which was encouraging to me, for so many of us hoped the war would be over by Christmas, so we could spend time with our beloved families.

I believe that my most difficult duty was to get them to pipe down about their adventures so that they could eat the hearty meals of beef and potatoes we served them. This was one of the best hospitals I've had the privilege to work at as there was always a bed for anyone who needed it, and I often played card games with the soldiers for good fun.

However, there was a war on, and occasionally, shells would land in the nearby fields. Nobody was ever hurt; usually, the shells missed houses and instead killed unfortunate livestock. For obvious safety reasons, we soon relocated the hospital to a nearby village. While there, I even met a young man, a soldier by the name of Luther Baker, who had overcome a mental deficiency just so that he could serve his country as a soldier. A fine soldier he was, too. To his mother, who undoubtedly is reading this, please know I am doing all I can to look after him. If the news I receive is true, the war should be over very soon, thanks to the boldness and excellent morale of the British Expeditionary Force, and our dear Luther will be on his way home a hero.

Ryan Byrnes

To Ethyl Brand,

Congratulations! I received your article and thought it was a wonderful piece of journalism. I will publish it in the upcoming week. Thank you for considering the Leamington Courier. *Please write more; I feel you will attract a great audience.*
Also, I do in fact know your family. Your father and I went to school together when we were lads. Funny thing, how small the world is.
Attached is your payment.

Sincerely,
Mr. Michael Surrey
The Leamington Courier

CHRISTMAS EVE, 1914
THE WESTERN FRONT

~ THE FRONT ~

The soldiers passed around cigarettes and sang angry songs. They were all rookies; only ten veterans remained from August. Tom was gone. Appleby was gone. Coffee Can Stoker was gone. Wallace, Wright, Somers, and Nash were gone. There were not enough soldiers left to teach the new boys, who arrived younger and shorter and scrawnier by the day. Food was running short because a shell punched the commissary into the earth, so they roasted rats over fires.

"I need to eat something green; that's all I want."

"I want to see my sweetheart. Soon's I get back, I'm marrying her. Don't care what her old man says."

"I want to sit by the fire with my dog and a mug of good beer."

"They can't treat people like this. We need to start a union."

"A union? It's a war, for God's sake."

"What's a union called during a war, then?"

"A mutiny."

They fell silent.

"The Germans don't want to fight either. The trenches are so close that I was talking with one of them about football the other day."

"Seems only the officers want to fight. Why can't they work it out on their own time?"

"What if we all just stopped fighting? What if we just refused?"

"That's daft. No man would drop his gun when a thousand others are aiming at him."

Silence again.

"When do you think Luther will come 'round?" He motioned over to the flooded dugout where they used to keep the radio. Inside, the white mud was frozen hard, and a dark figure crouched in the corner.

"No idea. I tried talking to him, but all he does is sit there curled up and stiff. He's not even doing that rocking thing. Or rolling the mud into those damn little balls. Think he's lost the will."

"Was he wounded?"

"Just shook up. Spent the whole night in a crater with Stoker."

"Shell shock. Poor bloke." The others nodded. "Never should have been here in the first place."

Captain Blanding emerged from his bunker in the reserve trench, his boots squeaking in the mud. After wishing each soldier a Happy Christmas Eve with a hearty handshake, he told them their attack would begin at sunrise. One man, who'd been grumbling while cleaning his bayonet, stood up and threw his rifle to the ground.

"I'm gonna die either way," he declared to his friends as he drew his arm back and slugged the surprised captain in the jaw. "May as well die on my own terms." The captain stumbled back and then steadied himself while the soldier rubbed his knuckles and waited for the fall out.

"Guards!" Blanding roared, and two armed men appeared and escorted the slugger away. The captain took a deep breath and straightened the lapels of his coat. "Men, we must remember this fight is bigger than you and me," he said with his refined Oxford accent. "This is for king and country. For hearth and home. We have to put duty first, so I implore you to take heart. The Germans are hurting. If we break through their line tomorrow morning, the river valley will be ours. Just think. We'll be victorious on Christmas Day just as you promised your families. Face this day with courage, ready yourselves like greyhounds in the slips—"

The men drowned his words in a low chorus of *boo's* and *pssh's*.

"Who does he think he is, telling me we'll win the war tomorrow?"

"Is he quoting Shakespeare?"

Blanding was calm. With hands clasped behind his back, he scanned the huddled soldiers causing dissension in the ranks, and identified the three loudest voices. He called again for the guards and in moments two men bearing military police insignia appeared and dragged three men away.

"This is what you signed up for," the captain proclaimed to the men who remained. "I have my own orders straight from the General, and they are to see that any man who actively opposes the war effort at this crucial time is shot for treason."

Before the men had time to react, a gunshot sounded, and they all dove for cover, including Captain Blanding.

◆❖◆

In the formerly idyllic village of Estaires, a British soldier and three little girls stepped over the threshold of the church and, in the glow of dozens of flickering candles, joined the families—wrapped tight in coats and gloves and scarves—packed close together. Sons and daughters tucked between mothers and fathers, who touched hands and gazed at each other, marveling at the bubble they had created between themselves. That bubble, the bubble of childhood, depended upon love and luck and was a gift unevenly shared. Sometimes the bubble would burst without a sound before it could be noticed. Knowing this, tears stung at the eyes of congregants as they sang of comfort and joy while the organ moaned and whispered through the notched pipes.

Outside, breath misted beneath the stars. Inside, the air was close and vibrated with hymns that were full and deep, wafting softly across the banners of purple cloth, wreaths of aromatic evergreen, old tweed, and new wool sheared off the lamb. The priest read about the babe that slept in straw, the lamb of God, and spoke of virtue and kindness great enough to persist through trial and tribulation yet small enough to make the tiniest child smile and sigh in delight.

The candle flames fluttered on their wicks, glinting off of the gold chalice the priest raised high, his hands tremoring with age. Chanted Latin echoed off of the walls. The people bowed their heads. They did not know Latin, and many could not read the hymns out of the song books, but they would sing from habit, nodding and smiling and thinking the same thoughts they had been trained to think every Sunday of their lives. They did not know the long history of kings and conquerors and wars beyond their village walls, but took comfort in the legacy of the earth beneath their feet, the grandmothers and grandfathers, the mothers and sons, and the fathers and daughters.

The organ spiked an octave, and the priest paced down the aisle with folded hands, passing under the gazes of various statues, plaster faces of anguish and majesty and hope. There was the Virgin Mary adorned with poinsettias, head bowed and arms framed in her drooping blue robes. There were Saints Peter and Paul, with the protruding beards of philosophers and sharp brows and hard pointed noses that seemed to smell the curling incense rising, the sweet soapy balsam of frankincense softening the air. The priest swung the clinking gold chain of the incense, and the song swelled as the people hummed the "*Douce Nuit*," the silent night, the holy night, where all is calm and all is bright.

When the priest left, so did most of the people. They nudged their children awake and led or carried them out under the stars. When they arrived home and closed and locked their front doors, they'd find embers still glowing in the hearth next to the shoes that had been laid out.

The children would scramble quickly to the fire, extinguishing it so that Peré Noël would not burn himself on his way down the chimney. The stairs pounded with little feet racing to bed so that Peré Noël would not pass them over. Doors slammed shut, bedsprings squeaked once, and there was no sound after that.

Back at the church, lights flickered out. Inside, the priest changed out of his robes and hung them in the closet. He blew out all of the candles, except those for the dead—those candles would be kept burning bright. He knelt before the cross and prayed for an end to the war, and when he turned, he saw the British soldier and three little girls waiting patiently for him to finish. After exchanging a few words, for the priest knew English, the girls were shown to the donated mattresses laid out along the walls where other bundled refugees and beggars prepared to take their rest.

The girls, whose heads swayed as they slept-walked, collapsed onto the bedding. They tried to ignore the sound of their stomach's growling as the soldier whispered to them of ice skating and magical snowmen and pulled a blanket, a coat, and an oilcloth out of his duffle bag. He unfurled the cloth over them, taking care to tuck in the loose ends until they were bundled. As he worked, the girls looked up at him through drooping, slow-moving eyelids. The youngest girl was nestled in the middle, between her two older sisters, and she stared at the candles for the dead and the shining wax that dripped off of them. Her eyes were wet.

"Don't be sad," the soldier whispered.

Reaching into his bag, he pulled out a leather doll of a bearded man in a red coat.

"Don't forget this," he said, handing it to her, and she took it, and buried her face in the doll's red coat.

"*Non Peré Noël*," she whispered.

The soldier sat on a chair next to the girls and stared at the doll. He checked his watch and realized he must leave soon. He had mail to deliver. "Bernadette," he rested a hand on her forehead as her eyes fluttered. "Peré Noël wants you to sleep well."

She managed a small smile and closed her eyes to sleep, or at least to pretended to sleep. The girls had laid their shoes out by their mattresses—six little leather shoes set in a tidy line. The shoes were empty. Reaching into his bag once more, the soldier pulled out two stacks of bronze boxes that he set in each shoe. The boxes were adorned with engraved laurels and pillars, entitled CHRISTMAS 1914.

Inside, he knew there were little butterscotch sweets and pencils and paper for drawing. He'd taken out the cigarettes and stuffed them in his pocket where they might come in handy. The soldier glanced at his watch again but still did not leave his chair. He remained to watch their slow breathing in the candle light and understood that he felt what his own father must have felt when he was a babe. Before his father died. Before the hardships of loss and loneliness and Luther. He sighed deeply and wiped his eyes. These little girls were like royalty, too special to be trusted with any other guardian, and his own needs melted away in comparison.

He felt he must work for them, he must rise to their expectations, he must be better.

If only he could return the next morning.

Finally, he rose. He allowed himself one last backward glance and stepped outside. The lorry grumbled to life and the headlights swept through the stained glass as he turned down the road to Ploegsteert.

"Who fired that shot?" the officer called out.

"They've erected something, sir!" one of the snipers called from his post. "The Germans! Several somethings, along the trench line!"

The captain took the binoculars and called the men to their defensive positions. They imagined the Germans preparing artillery, screwing on their bayonets, loading their guns. They scrambled to their posts before the shells came, waking up their neighbors and calling out orders to inferiors. Some soldiers descended into the flooded dugout to collect ammunition. Luther still sat curled up in the corner. He never even looked up.

Looking through the binoculars, the Lieutenant spied the pointed helmets bobbing behind the German line, illumed by fires. Tall, dark shapes sprung up for a hundred meters in both directions. The sniper that sat beside the captain selected his ammunition with care and squinted at the shapes through one eye. *Crack.* One of them fell.

The soldiers shouted amongst themselves when the dark shapes began to sparkle with lights. The Germans held candles to them, and the fronds glowed green. Christmas trees.

While they all watched, two gloveless hands raised a sign out of the enemy trench. HAPPY CHRISTMAS, said the painted letters.

"It's a ruse," the captain grumbled, then shouted to the soldiers to hold still.

The sniper pressed his trigger, and the bullet snapped the air. The sign exploded into wood shards.

The Germans were quick to retaliate with song, and their voices swelled, hearty, and full of longing.

Wir sind drei Könige aus dem Morgenland,
Bringen Gaben aus der Ferne,
Über Feld und Quelle, Moor und Berg
Folgen wir jenem Stern.

Oh Stern des Wunders, Stern der Nacht,
Stern mit heller königlicher Schönheit,
Westwärts führend, weiter voran,
Führe uns zu deinem vollkommenen Licht.

The British soldiers mouthed the words in return. They still held onto their guns, glancing at their neighbors for assurance.

We three Kings of Orient are
Bearing gifts; we traverse afar,
Field and fountain, moor and mountain
Following yonder star.

Ooooo–oooo star of wonder, star of night,
Star with royal beauty bright,
Westward leading, still proceeding,
Guide us to thy perfect light.

One after another, Christmas carols echoed over the field and into the dugout where Luther clutched his knees. A choir of soldiers singing in German and English sang through the night as Luther tilted his head up to the starlight and felt warmth return to his bones.

~ ETHYL BRAND ~

The hospital in Hazebrouck was usually full, but on Christmas Eve there were ten empty beds. Fancy that. That morning, we had shipped off the most recent batch of wounded to Calais by train, and nobody came to fill the beds. I took advantage of the break and headed to the doctor's lounge, a tile room with a few chairs, a coffee grinder, and some playing cards. I checked my mailbox for any letters from High Command, a response to Luther's medical evaluation, permission for him to finally go home. Nothing of the sort. Maybe tomorrow. I poured myself a cup of coffee and sank into a wooden chair.

"What do you suppose is going on out there?" One of the nuns had followed me into the lounge. It was almost midnight, and I longed for some sleep. Instead of bed, I sat at the table, sweeping up the untidy pile of cards and bridging them for solitaire.

"Couldn't tell you," I shrugged. "I heard shells and gunfire up until last night, when it all stopped. Less firepower and less wounded, all on Christmas Eve. Think I like the sound of that."

"The men are in good spirits. We have a battalion billeted in the village—you may not have heard gunfire, but I heard plenty of drunken shouting. Apparently, they're putting on a play—*A Christmas Carol* or something like that."

"The soldiers are putting it on? I wonder who's playing the female characters."

"The men, I supposed. A regular Globe Theatre, I guess."

"Would you like to see it after our shift? I hear they're doing another performance later today," the nun said.

"I believe I would." I downed my coffee and splashed another cupful into the mug. The nun scratched her chin as she studied the cards laid out before her, carefully drawing from the piles and stacking them.

"Ethyl, sometimes I watch you and I notice how quiet you are, even when all the others are losing their heads. Sometimes I get the feeling you don't care anymore. Do you think this is all futile, what we're doing here in this hospital? I mean, we fix the soldiers up just so they can go back."

Her eyes flickering over to me and then back to her coffee.

"Strange question for a woman of God to ask." I took another sip, and the nun waited.

"There is a tribe in Africa that lives along banks of the Niger River," I began. "According to their mythology, the Creator intended for them to be immortal, so he sent a dog from heaven to reveal the secret of eternal life. However, the dog was lazy and took a nap in the forest, and the Creator instead had to send a lamb as his messenger. The lamb journeyed to the tribe quickly, but the lamb forgot the message and changed the words. They believed the lamb. The next day, the dog arrived and told everyone the true message. They did not believe the dog. For this reason, the tribe never attained immortality, and the secret was lost forever."

The nun laid her cards down.

"So you're saying that we should spend more time listening to lazy people who run late?"

I shrugged.

Outside, a rubber horn *awooga'd* and the daily ambulance grumbled to a stop at the front doors. I sighed. So much for seeing the play. If there were injured needing transport from the front to the hospital, one of us nurses usually accompanied the driver to pick up the wounded.

"Mother Brand! Mother Brand!" A pimpled Red Cross volunteer appeared at the door. "I've got word that a patrol of soldiers near Ploegsteert was hit by a shell. One of the survivors is asking for you. He's in bad shape, but says you must settle your debt to him, though I'm not quite sure what that means."

"His name?"

"Rodney Stoker."

I grabbed my coat off the rack as I rushed out the door. "Take me to him."

CHRISTMAS DAY, 1914
THE WESTERN FRONT

~ THE FRONT ~

As the pink of dawn brushed the horizon, the soldiers fell silent. Waiting. It was Christmas Day.

Luther rose.

The men saw him emerge from his hidey hole and whispered to each other. Like a prisoner at the execution, like a priest at the procession, he hobbled toward the ladder leading to No Man's Land.

"Luther—you alright?"

"Where're you off to, Luther?"

Luther approached the edge of the trench and stood on the ladder. Several voices flared up.

"Get down from there!"

"The Germans will shoot!"

"Someone grab him!"

They rushed to grab him, but he had already climbed halfway. His legs trembled as he hugged the ladder, whimpering.

"Stand down!" Captain Blanding called.

Luther looked back at him.

"Do not disobey your superior!" Captain Blanding's voice cracked for the first time.

Luther lifted himself onto the next rung.

Captain Blanding pulled out his pistol, but Luther rolled over the top and scrambled to his feet. He raised his hands above his head and stepped over the frozen bodies, sobbing as he went. Now that he had gone, the soldiers fell silent and tracked his movements with open mouths and wide eyes, whispering secret words of encouragement.

Luther stepped over the barbed wire, shuddering as he passed the fallen Appleby, now shiny with frost. A white down had settled on the bodies; they looked like pearly mounds, misshapen pieces of toffee dusted with sugar. And from some unseen heaven, snow floated down to Earth, and the flakes caught in Luther's hair, his eyelashes, his beard, and fluttered down to perch on his shoulders and kiss his tear-stained red cheeks. No Man's Land was desolate and beautiful and, like the scene within a child's snow globe, was enameled with sparkling ice and gently falling snow.

From the German side, a pointed helmet rose to reveal a mustached face. On the British side, the men shuddered, wishing Luther farewell. But then the German climbed out, too.

"Shoot him," Captain Blanding ordered the snipers.

The guns remained quiet.

The German was wearing a long coat with tails that blew behind him like a magician in a fairy tale. His gloves were fingerless, and he carried no gun. By the time he reached the center of No Man's Land, he stopped, face to face with Luther. On both sides, legions of soldiers leaned in close to hear the words they exchanged, but nobody could make them out. The soldiers each watched their neighbors for guidance, unsure if the social boundaries still held sway. They searched each other's eyes for a spark, for a sign that this moment, this day, would be different.

Another Brit climbed out of the trench, and his neighbor saw the spark and knew he must climb out, too.

Luther and the German shook hands.

Mum and Dad,

Happy Christmas! We are enjoying our Christmas at the front much more than I'd anticipated, for this was surely a day I will remember even when I am an old man.

Believe it or not, I met a Fritz today. The soldiers saw fit to drop their guns and celebrate good will for Christmas, so we all headed out into the battlefield with the agreement that nobody would shoot until at least Boxing Day, New Year's if we're lucky. We shook hands and passed around some tobacco. I traded ten cigarettes for a German helmet, which I am sending back to you in the post as a keepsake. One of the Brits managed to lash together a football out of some medical tape and newspapers, and we had a good kickabout with the Germans. Nobody kept score, but it was a nice break from being shot at all day long.

Thank you for your gift. The dry socks have left me in good spirits, and I look forward to seeing you after my service is up.

With love,
George

Dearest Susanna,

My, what a wonderful Christmas this has turned out to be! A spontaneous truce has broken out between us and the Huns, and I found myself this morning hung over in the German trench, a roast mutton in one hand. I thought all this time the Germans were starving, but they have been living like lords compared to us. They have bread and sausage every day, and beer is always available. I have never met a more cheerful group.

This morning, I chatted with a chap named Friedrich. He was born in Saxony and then went to live with his uncle in London, where he worked as a bellboy at the Grand Trafalgar Hotel. We talked some politics about Parliament and our hopes for the next PM, and I'd say he's a pretty straight fellow. We exchanged addresses so that when the war ends, we can visit each other's families.

Susanna, how I love your name! Your gift made me teary-eyed and filled me with warm strength. I cannot say how much you mean to me—my memories of you have compelled me to survive and cooled my fears in times of chaos. Imagine I am in your arms.

I will return to you.
Charlie

Uncle Jacob,

You once spoke to me of honor and discipline, and I heeded your words. Keep this letter somewhere safe because you may need to procure it before a military court. The facts are, I have become entangled in a mutiny of my peers. All along the front, Brits have thrown away their guns and are fraternizing with the enemy. It started on Christmas Eve, when the Huns started caroling, and a mad romantic got the idea in his head to walk out into the field and join them for a song and a drink! They proceeded to engage in drunken celebration and general ruckus throughout the night. In the morning, when they woke around noon from their hangovers, they fashioned a football out of rubbish and started an organized match. My fellows pressed me hard to participate; they wanted me to help bury the dead and clear the battlefield for a football pitch. I give you my word that I heartily refused and remained in the bunker with my commanders. Some of my fellow troops even considered deserting, and I was quick to remind them the punishment for desertion is death.

More letters will be coming soon.
Sincerely,
Vincent

Ryan Byrnes

Dear Grandmother,

Happy Christmas! Today has shown me that there is some good left in the human race; it refuses to fade. I have fared better than most in the combat, for the thought of little Jenny motivates me. Tell Jenny that her father is safe and sound and that Santa Claus visited the troops. We all decided to forget the war for a little bit and exchanged gifts with the Germans! They really are decent gentlemen, which strikes me as funny since just the other day we behaved like animals toward each other. I've managed to ride my bicycle over behind the German lines and do a bit of exploring. I swore to them I wasn't a spy, which was good enough. They invited me to drink in their officers' bunker, a rather spacious fortress, but I politely refused because I was afraid high command would find out and arrest me for treason. Besides, I'm not much of a drinking man, and you know that!

Anyhow, I am sending Jenny a gift of sweets that all of the soldiers received from the Princess. Tell her I am glad that she has behaved well and received high marks in her studies.

God Bless,
James

~ JIM BAKER ~

Dawn blazed white in the vales and turnip farms near Ploegsteert Wood. Ice glimmered on the telegraph lines, the barbed wire, the radio antennae; it filled in the cracks in concrete pillboxes where the steel beams were once exposed. The crusty charred faces of brick walls and gashed tree trunks were masked, and all sharp angles and hard edges softened under the pressure of sloping drifts.

Only the roads did not sparkle. They were dark and muddy, and the deep-rutted tire tracks had churned up the snow into half-melted slush that *slosh sloshed* for every passing vehicle, like my post lorry that grumbled down the road, the engine grill spitting out a shimmering mirage that had fumed for hours, for miles, nonstop all through the night between villages. I pulled up next to the reserve trenches where the beasts of artillery loomed, their massive iron nozzles plugged with snow. I opened the door and stepped out, boots sinking into the slush. Knowing the old lorry might not restart in the cold, I left the engine running and headed down the causeway into the trench, where the entrances to the dugouts and pillboxes were anointed with wreaths. I heard shouts in the distance and saw an ambulance on the flat horizon, but no gunshots split the day.

"Hello?" I called, and only the swirling flurries answered.

No answer, but in the distance, I heard shouts and cheers.

Peeking inside a dugout, I saw empty beds and crates of ammunition.

I crunched through the snow. I passed into the next ring of trenches—the frontline that looked out on the turnip field. It, too, was empty. The din was louder, though, and I glanced up at the edge of the trench, just above my head. I trembled as I approached the ladder, climbed up, and poked my head over the top.

"Good God."

No Man's Land was flat and clean. The bodies that I'd heard lay unclaimed for days or weeks had been removed, and the tangles of barbed wire were smoothed over with snow. Men laughed and ran and grabbed each other by the shoulder. Some lucky bloke had procured a leather ball for a kickabout. German and Brit played football like old friends, cupping the ball with their feet and sending it flying with wide kicks that they *step step stepped* into, the ball sailing high with a spray of snow. They gave hearty handshakes and spit tobacco while legions of snowmen wearing scarves and medals and pointed helmets watched from the sidelines and two boys tackled each other into the drifts while others lounged nearby, playing cards or writing letters. One of the Germans sat while a Brit lathered his sideburns in foam, shaving him clean with a razor. Another napped against a snowman, hands folded peacefully.

I exhaled. The cruelty of the world fell away. *Sometimes, sweetness survives*, I thought. But Luther was nowhere to be seen.

"Luther!" I cupped my hands and sent his call over the field. A couple of the men noticed and waved at me. "Luther Baker!"

I climbed the ladder and went out to meet the soldiers. "I'm looking for Luther Baker. Know him?"

They laughed. "Luther—the man who lives in No Man's Land? The one who started this whole thing? Sure we know him!"

"How do you mean?"

They slapped me on the back and handed me a cooked chicken leg. "We were due to start another offensive, but Luther, God bless him, just climbed up out of the trench, marched over toward the German line, and shook hands with a Hun. Merry Christmas, indeed!"

"Where is he now?" I asked.

"He was playing football with us just a moment ago." The two men looked around, squinting into the sunlight. "There he is!"

In the midst of the football kickabout, my big brother squatted on his hams, rolling truffles out of snow. Thank you, God, Zeus, Buddha, whoever it was out there pulling the strings. My brother was safe.

"Luther?"

He rose from his truffles upon hearing my voice. He trembled where he stood as I ran toward him.

"Luther!"

I clamped my arms around his blood-stained khaki, holding him close until his trembling turned to strength.

"Little brother," he shivered into my shoulder while I dusted the snow out of his hair and off his uniform. He stunk of every bodily fluid I could imagine, a fair helping of smoke on top of that.

"Are you hurt at all?" I asked, searching him up and down for cuts. He had winced when I hugged him, suggesting hurt ribs. His eyes were sunken in dark bags, most frightful of all.

"Merry Christmas," was all I could say before pulling him in again for another hug.

I'd never hugged anybody that long before. And he'd never let me hug him before at all. More and more soldiers stared. Not wanting to attract attention before I made our getaway, I guided Luther back through the trenches, past the bunkers, and the beasts of artillery.

"How did you come here?" Luther asked.

I hadn't much time for greetings. I had a strict plan, and this was the perfect time to execute it, while everyone was distracted by the truce.

"Take this," and I stuffed some papers into his hands. "And don't show them to anyone."

"What are these?" Luther squinted at them.

"Tickets to Algeria. You're leaving this hell hole."

~ ETHYL BRAND ~

Snow-buried fields sailed past, and while the ambulance driver squinted into the flurries, I sat in the passenger seat, working the hand-crank siren until my wrist was sore, then switching to the other hand.

"Out of the way!" I stuck my head out the window and called to some mule carts.

We swerved around them; my nurse's cap flew off my head and vanished behind me. The engine growled and sputtered black smoke out the tailpipe as the frontline sliced the horizon. I squinted at its radiance—a fresh dusting of snow had rendered the mire pure as opal.

Screech. The ambulance kicked up an arc of sludge, and I leapt out. The medics manning the auxiliary trenches had Rodney waiting for us. Rodney was wrapped tight in a blanket, but I picked up and edge and peeked under it. His uniform hung in shreds off his skin. His face shone red, crusted over with black dirt and gold pus. He reeked of smoke. Someone had already bandaged his hand, his chest, and one of his thighs. They'd done a decent job.

Rodney moaned and mumbled as we loaded him in the ambulance.

I bent over his stretcher. "Is Luther safe?"

The burnt husk of a man didn't respond, so I shouted the words until his mouth moved. I leaned in to hear his words.

"Free from fear."

"Luther," I repeated. "Is he safe?"

"Alive … in danger."

"Where is he?"

"No Man's Land," he whispered.

"What?"

But he fell silent. I felt his pulse. Weak, but still beating.

"Keep cruising!" I shouted for the ambulance driver. "There's a second soldier who needs treatment."

"Where to?"

"I don't know! He said 'No Man's Land.'"

The driver slammed his foot on the pedal, and the ambulance's canvas covering flapped as we sped parallel with the trenches. I squinted out the window through the raw sunlight reflecting off the snow, looking for Luther. Stretching out before us was a moonscape—rubble heaps tall as a house and craters just as deep. The ambulance smashed through a fence, rattling my bones. Rodney winced, but he didn't even have the strength to scream. Why'd they make these ambulances so cheap? They had the shock absorption of a wheelbarrow. There was nothing else I could do for Rodney other than roll up my coat as a cushion under his head. We needed to get him back to the hospital fast. But not without Luther.

"What's that brewing over there?" the driver shouted over the rumbling engine.

"How do you mean?"

"Have a look," he pointed. "See that ruckus down there?"

I followed his gaze to the pearly turnip fields, now crawling with soldiers.

"Are they—are they playing football?"

"Looks like Trafalgar Square!"

Our eyes met and the driver gave me a bright laugh. "Has the King called for a ceasefire or something?" he asked. "I never got the news."

"*What is it?*" Rodney mumbled.

"The fighting's stopped," I said. "I can't explain it. They're making snowmen and playing cards and sharing rations. I can't explain it."

He stirred. "I must be in heaven."

~ JIM BAKER ~

"Climb in, Luther," I pointed into the back of the mail lorry, where I had emptied a large cargo crate with lid just for him.

"I don't want to."

"Just get in the crate," I pointed. "Now."

Luther stood there with his arms crossed and a petulant frown on his face. "What's Algeria and why do I have tickets for it?"

"I'm taking you to see Mum."

After I invoked Mum, Luther climbed into the crate without another word, and I shut it over him. I wasn't a mean brother; Luther had been enthralled with small spaces his whole life. Back at home, he'd take naps regularly in the cupboard. I spun around to check if any blokes had watched the scene play out. The coast was clear; all the soldiers were occupied with the truce. Perfect distraction, too. A ruddy miracle, if I'd ever seen one.

I slipped into the driver's seat and gripped the wheel. My hands shook so much that I wondered if I'd be able to steer. I had left the lorry running because I wasn't sure if it would restart in this cold.

Vroom vroom vroom.

Slowly, we rolled through the slush, gathering speed as the site of the No Man's Land truce shrank behind us. My stomach churned even though I'd barely eaten. I kept looking around to make sure nobody was watching us. Luther shifted around in the back of the truck.

"Cut the clatter back there! Just a little farther and we'll be in the clear."

A chorus of giggles replied. Not Luther's giggles, but little girls' giggles. A foot to the brake pedal sent me lurching forward. I pulled over to the side of the road, flung open my door, and marched around to the back of the lorry.

"Where the bloody hell are they?"

I made a pigsty of the truckbed, spilling mail sacks all over until I found them. Three little girls curled up in the corner with their Santa Claus dolls, cheeks full of toffee. The Moreau sisters—Celeste, Bernadette, and Adele. They had made a festivity of picking over the shiny Christmas boxes intended for the troops, shaking out every morsel of candy, piling the empty boxes at their feet.

"*Peré Noël!*" they greeted me.

Celeste offered me a chunk of toffee.

"I told you to stay at the church," I chucked the toffee in the snow. "How did you even manage to sneak in the truck? Do you have any idea how dangerous this is?"

Not only did I have to get Luther to Algeria, but now I had to deal with these girls, too. While I lectured them,

Adele snuck a piece of toffee to Luther. He slipped it in his mouth, and a smile broke over his face.

"You've had enough sweets for today," I snatched up an armful of the brass Christmas boxes from them, tried to stuff mail back into the sacks, and yelled at Luther to get back in the lorry. As I gathered handfuls of mail, a letter caught my eye, and I held it up. It was the same letter I'd seen on the train. The official looking one addressed to Ethyl Brand. *Ethyl Brand!*

"Someone's coming!" Luther yelled and clapped his hands over his ears. I turned to see an ambulance careening straight at us.

I shoved the letter back in the sack, pointed my finger at the girls, and hissed, "Hide!"

~ ETHYL BRAND ~

I couldn't believe my eyes. "*Stop!* That's Luther!"

The ambulance driver slammed the breaks, and Rodney's stretcher slid in the back. I knew I was risking Rodney's life. I promised him I'd get him the best care. But I wasn't heading back to the hospital without Luther.

I hopped out of the ambulance, onto the snow sludge, approaching the pulled-over mail lorry. I'd never seen a mail lorry just parked on the side of the road. A flat tire, perhaps? But what on earth was Luther doing there? How had he gotten away from his unit? I thought he was injured. I couldn't make sense of it, but a nagging thought caught me off guard. Desertion. No! Luther was coming to the hospital with me, I would treat him for his wounds, we would receive his letter of leave, and he'd be sent on his way home. Officially. Not as a criminal. That would not do. When I walked to the rear of the lorry, I gasped. Luther crouched inside a wooden crate, three little girls poked their heads from behind mountains of post sacks, and directing the whole fiasco: Jim Baker.

Jim Baker?

"Having a little family reunion, are we?"

Jim froze. Then he slowly turned around.

"Ethyl?"

He was a mess—dark circles under his eyes, stubble shading his neck and jaw, hair blowing every which way in the fluttering snowfall.

"So the rumors are true," I crossed my arms. "You did become a bum after all. What are you doing with this truck? Who are these girls? Why is Luther in that crate?"

"We're going to Algeria to see Mum," Luther piped up, climbing back out of the crate and jumping down to stand beside Jim.

"*Algeria?*"

"I know what you're thinking," Jim held out his hands as if in surrender. "Seems like Switzerland would be the natural choice, right? Turns out, Algeria is actually the best—"

"You jolly well know that's beside the point. If you and Luther are caught, you'll both be court-martialed for desertion. Blokes get executed for that shite. You know what execution is, right? Or should I explain it to you?"

At the word *execution*, Luther looked to Jim for guidance. Why did Jim get the final say-so? I'm the one who'd been looking after Luther. I'm the one who had calmed his tears, arranged to get him tested by physicians, and written letters on his behalf. And now he was looking to Jim for advice?

"Luther, you're coming with me. Are you hurt?"

"Don't listen to her, Luther," Jim stepped in his way. "You want to see Mum, right?"

"Oh please," I crossed my arms. "Luther was already going to see his mum. His letter of leave should arrive in the post any day now. In fact, the letter's probably in one of these post sacks you're carrying."

"Letter of leave?" Jim paused. "What's this about a letter of leave?"

"I arranged for several doctors to conduct a formal assessment of Luther. Like any sane person, each one concluded he's not fit for combat, that there was a mistake in enlistment, and recommended he be sent home. I compiled their reports and sent them to headquarters. I'm just waiting for the official letter."

"That's a damn good plan," Jim said, more to himself than to me.

"Of course, it's a damn good plan." I turned to Luther. "How does that sound," I said. "Ready to go home?"

"I want to go see Mum."

"I know you do," I said. Then I turned back to Jim. "And what are you doing with three little girls? And how did you get a hold of this truck?" Ethyl eyed me up and down. "Did you really enlist?"

"I'm delivering mail to the troops," Jim said, "and these girls seem to have decided I'm Santa Claus. They're refugees. Discovered them hiding in the train from Le Havre."

"And what are they doing in your—"

"What's going on here?" I turned to see a mounted military police officer riding toward us. Bloody hell. I shot Jim a warning glance and started toward them, trying to block Luther from their sight.

"I've got an injured soldier in the ambulance," I said, "but we stopped to see if this lorry driver needed help."

"What is it? A flat tire?" The MMP looked at Jim's lorry and then dismounted. That's when he saw Luther. "Private? What are you doing here?"

Jim swore.

"Don't you say a word," I hissed at him. "I'm doing the talking."

~ JIM BAKER ~

In seconds, Celeste and her sisters had managed to tuck themselves away in the mail sacks, but Luther was just standing there right out in the great outdoors. My first instinct was to throw Luther in the back, slam the gas pedal, and make a run for it. But my first instincts weren't known for turning out so great. I'd be putting both Luther and the girls in danger. Ethyl grabbed my wrist in an iron grip, holding me fast.

"If I have to sacrifice you to save Luther and those three girls, I will," she whispered.

The MMP stepped past me to look inside the truck. Luckily the girls were smart enough to stay hidden. He turned to Luther. "A sad day for the war," he said. "Peace has broken out. Unauthorized truces have been bastardized. The day is rank with fraternization, and what's more, it appears, desertion."

"It's not desertion," Luther said, pulling out the ticket I gave him. "I'm going to Algeria to see Mum. I have a ticket."

In a flash, the MMP had pulled his pistol and had it expertly trained on my big brother. Without thinking I stepped between the MMP and Luther, whose eyes had widened at the site of the gun pointed right at him.

The officer studied Luther from his boots to the top of his head, and then snatched the ticket from his hand. "How does a Royal Warwickshire private come across a ticket to Algeria? He's found in the company of a post-man, a nurse, and—" he strolled over to peer in Ethyl's ambulance. "Driver," he called, "open these doors!"

The driver climbed out of the ambulance and opened the back doors. A body lay on a stretcher inside.

"Who is this?"

Ethyl stepped up. "Rodney Stoker of the Royal War-wickshires. Severely injured in yesterday's battle."

My God. Rodney? He was unrecognizable.

"Is he dead?" the MMP asked.

"Not if I can help it. I need to get him to the hospital immediately."

"And yet you stopped to help a post lorry that, it appears, does not need your help. Sounds logical."

He turned back to the lorry. And to Luther and me.

"You all are going to need to step away from the lorry," the officer said. My knees buckled. He poked around in the driver's seat and the passenger's seat, and started to climb up in the back. He would find Celeste and her sisters at any moment. Love letters and Christmas greet-ings fluttered from the open sacks like autumn leaves. I knew I needed to distract them, but I was frozen to the spot.

"Excuse me," Ethyl called, and the officer turned from the girls' hiding spot. "Private Baker is on his way home to Warwickshire, and we stopped to see him because he was injured with Private Stoker and wanted to say farewell to his brother-in-arms. Private Baker has permission to leave. Medical leave. There was a mistake in enlistment, you see. A mix-up. I'm getting papers to prove he is not capable of serving. He's, uh, he's different. Differently abled, and—"

"Differently abled?" the MMP scoffed. "What's this rubbish?"

"It's a doctor's diagnosis," Ethyl huffed. "His brain does not work the way yours or mine does."

The MMP held out his hand. "Show me the papers then," he demanded.

"I … I don't have the papers. Yet. I'm expecting them any day."

"Sure you are."

Ethyl was trying hard to keep her cool. "His papers are coming in the post! I swear it."

Hang on, I thought. *I'm the postman, aren't I?* And didn't I just see a letter addressed to Ethyl Brand? The same official-looking letter I'd seen on the train? Blimey. I'd just stuffed the envelope back into one of the bags! I just need to find it.

"That's a great story, Miss, but you're going to have to stand down or you're going to end up under arrest, too." The MMP turned back to Luther and grabbed his arm. As soon as the officer touched him, he lost it. Hands flapping, moaning, rocking, the whole sordid bit.

"Luther, don't fight them," Ethyl folded her hands in prayer. "Please don't fight. Your letter will arrive soon. We'll work this out."

It was no use. Luther swung his fists and spun circles, startling the officer who tried to grab his hands again.

While they were distracted, I slipped into the lorry.

"*Oye!*" the officer called.

"Wait!" I shouted. "The letter is in here! I just saw it!" Where was it? I flipped through a few post sacks until I found the one marked for the hospital at Hazebrouck. I swore as I flipped through all the envelopes.

"Here! I have it. I found it!" I shouted as the officer dragged me out of the lorry. "The letter is right here. Here's your Christmas present, everyone."

Ethyl Brand, the letter was addressed.

The officer snatched it. For a second, I thought he would tear it to pieces. But, seeing the seal of high command, he paused.

Ethyl stepped forward and held out her hand. "That's my letter. That's Private Luther Baker's ticket home. And that's why I stopped to help the post lorry. I hoped that today, Christmas Day, the letter would come."

"This can't be real," the officer shook his head. He handed the letter to Ethyl and instructed her to open it and read it aloud. His eyes darted from me to Luther to Ethyl and over to the ambulance where the driver waited and Rodney was moaning. He double checked our dog tags. He asked for our identification papers. He took the letter from Ethyl and read it again. It was obviously the real deal. General Haig's signature was clear as day.

"So he's not right in the head?" he asked.

"I wouldn't say that at all," Ethyl frowned. "He's just different, and only in certain ways. He's the most brilliant candy maker you've ever seen. He's got more courage than anyone else I know. Jim here was sent to bring him back home to England."

"Bollocks," the officer snapped. "If he was going home to England, what's he doing with tickets to Algeria and hiding in the back of the lorry?"

That was a good point.

All heads turned toward me.

"Officer!" Rodney sputtered from his stretcher in the ambulance. "I did it."

What?

We all gravitated over to the ambulance where, injured as he was, Rodney was trying to sit up.

"I gave Luther the ticket. To smuggle him out. He shouldn't be here. Never should've been here."

"Rod, no," I whispered.

The officer, holding Luther's letter of leave in one hand, the ticket to Algeria in the other, peered down at Rodney.

"You're the man behind the smuggling?"

Rodney managed to incline his chin, evoking a nod.

"That's grounds for court martial," the officer said. He looked down at Rodney, then at the letter, and then at Luther. Finally, he released Luther.

"Get him out of here," Ethyl whispered to me. "You'd better be quick about it."

But Luther had bent down toward Rodney, and I joined him at Rodney's side.

"Are you still afraid of me, Rodney Stoker?" Luther asked.

"No," Rodney whispered. "You tried to save my life."

"Thank you for writing the letter for me to give to Mum. I still have it." Luther fished in his pocket and brought out a piece of paper with nothing but scribbling on it.

"I'm glad," Rodney whispered and closed his eyes.

I leaned over my former best friend. "Rod, I can't repay you for this," I said.

"We're square," Rodney's lips cracked in a sort of smile. "Visit my parents, will you? Tell them …" His voice faded. I ran back over to the lorry and pulled out the novel wedged in the front seat cushions. *A Tale of Two Cities*.

"Take this," I set it beside Rod. "As a Christmas gift."

"It is a far, far better thing that I do, than I have ever done," Rodney croaked. "It is a far better rest that I go to, than I have ever known before." He coughed, and then looked up at me through unseeing eyes. "Take Luther home, Jim. Eat some truffles for me."

With that, we left Rodney to the officer.

Crunching snow was the only sound. Luther and I stepped over to the still-rumbling lorry. He slammed the door in the passenger seat while the officers watched.

I don't know what nonsense it was that moved me, but I turned and blurted the damndest thing to Ethyl, "Come with us, Ethyl."

"Not a chance," she shook her head. "The war is still on, and my work isn't done. Besides, someone has to be here to take care of Rodney. Now go. Take care of Luther and those other precious packages in the back. I'll visit you from time to time, don't you worry."

"Right," I swallowed.

With that, I clicked the lorry door shut and gripped the icy steering wheel.

"Ready to go see Mum, big brother?" I nodded at Luther in the passenger seat.

"Yes, little brother," he smiled.

We cut through the snowy slush, gaining speed. Minutes later, the trench had faded from view. I'd later crack open the *Leamington Courier* to chuckle at the headline. *Soldiers Carry Christmas Truce into January.* I prayed that the snowmen enjoyed full, long lives in No Man's Land.

BOXING DAY, 1914
LEAMINGTON SPA, ENGLAND

~ CONSTANCE BAKER ~

Sleeping syrup befriended me in those months after Luther's enlistment. I had scarred the label with my fingernails but had not yet managed to tear it off. The label was the last thing I read before falling into bed at night. *Each ounce of this single-use syrup contains alcohol, cannabis, chloroform, and morphine to guarantee a good night's sleep.*

The grandfather clock *bong bong bonged* for noontime when I woke. My stomach growled for lunch or at least some chocolate, so I sat up, cradling my aching head. My vision spun, but just a little. I stared at the wall across my bed, remembering where Luther's crib used to sit. Before his passing, James would hum songs for Luther, lowering him into the crib. His side of the bed would be smooth and creaseless, while on my side all my tossing and turning had twisted the sheets into a rope.

When Luther was a baby, I would sometimes enter the room to see James sitting in the rocking chair, Luther in his arms, both snoring softly. I would remember the scene in the coming years. I would hoard it and become drunk on it. Then, three Christmases later, I would stand at the window and watch my husband leave on a trip to the grocery from which he would not return.

And now, twenty-five Christmases later, staring out the same window, I looked down into the empty street, dusted with snow, untouched by footprints. All down the street, the business had "closed" signs on the doors. Work halted for a day, and gift wrapping filled the rubbish bins of every house.

All except mine.

Lavinia said she would be checking in on me in the evening. She used that phrase a lot these days, "Check on you," like she was a doctor. She'd "checked in one me" Christmas morning, bringing me a gift I still hadn't opened. I'd gone right back upstairs and stayed in bed the rest of the day. What was the use? Without customers, I had no reason for dirtying the kitchen.

The day after Christmas, there'd be no business either. Good. I hadn't the energy or the will to go downstairs. I sighed and leaned my forehead against the windowpane. Wait. There, in the distance, a few souls wandered the street. Odd. I squinted, pulling at the blinds for a better view—two men trailed by three little girls. One of the men hoisted the smallest girl on his shoulders, while the other two girls danced circles in the snow. Their footsteps trailed behind them all the way down the street. They looked like they were headed for the shop. Didn't they know Christmas was already over? A few knocks rattled the door. At first, I didn't bother to go down and answer it, but they persisted.

"Your carols won't help me," I muttered, not nearly loud enough to be heard.

But still the knocks persisted.

Finally, I wrapped a sweater around my shoulders and pressed my feet onto the wood boards. At first, my legs wobbled, but I turned the doorknob to my bedroom and creaked down the freezing wood steps. The knocking persisted, this time from the back door, not the shop door like normal customers. Curious. I spotted their blurry outlines through the glazed windowpanes, and walked through the kitchen to open the back door.

"Love Mum!" two arms wrapped around me.

Crying out, I blacked out for a moment in Luther's arms. My head throbbed and my face glowed as blood rushed to my cheeks. Luther had brought others too—Jim and some little girls. I slammed the door behind them, locking it, but I couldn't fit the key in the lock on account of my trembling hands. None of them would ever leave this house again, never.

"Mum, it's okay," Jim took the key from me gently. "Nobody's after us. Luther's here to stay. Merry Christmas."

"Oh, James!" For the first time in years, I called him by his full name, his father's name. My son's name.

I clasped his cheeks, his nose, his chin, just like when he was a baby. Three white-haired, round-nosed little girls waved at me from the doormat. Their cheeks swelled with butterscotches.

"Who are they?" I asked.

There hadn't been a little girl in this house since Ethyl Brand twenty years ago.

"Mum, meet the Moreau sisters," Jim said. "Adele, Bernadette, and Celeste."

"*Bonjour Mère Noël*," the oldest said. "Is this North Pole?"

While the girls prattled on, Luther stared at the kitchen, boggle-eyed. He touched the handle of the cabinet that he would hide in after his tantrums, like an old friend. He didn't dare open it, just touched it. He continued to the flour sacks and the jars of sugar, powder sugar, cocoa powder, almonds. He touched the hanging spoons and whisks from his candy-making days. His footsteps wandered through the door, to the shop, behind the counter. Silent as a ghost, he stared through the glass at the fudge selection, the jars of rainbow bonbons, and finally, at the end of the counter, he came to the chocolate truffles.

I followed, watching him raise the truffles to his eyes, inspecting them slowly. And then he started weeping like a baby.

"*Mum.*"

I was able to do my job again. I held him tight until every tear dried. Luther's, mine, and even Jim's.

Luther would have nightmares the rest of his life. Candy making wasn't as fun for him anymore, but he still did it, mostly for the girls. He discovered in the Spring that Warwick Castle was still searching for a baker, and the job was his. We bought a bicycle, and he rode to work every day.

In the coming months, the sugar-fed giggling of the three girls bounced off the walls of the sweet shop. Santa dolls accumulated on the chocolate-bar shelves, and when the bells jingled over the door, happy customers asked me if they could try the best truffles in Europe. And when closing time came, I would lock up the door, clean the counters, and Lavinia would stroll by with the girls.

Lavinia, who was never able to have children, jumped at the chance to offer a room to the girls and quickly became a mother figure to them. We both did our best to make sure they felt at home, although Lavinia did her best to spoil them.

Jim returned to the frontlines shortly after Christmas, where he delivered mail to the troops for another three years. On the day he returned from France, he locked his uniform in a case under his bed and never opened it. Using his savings from his service, he moved into a brown-brick apartment in Warwick. The apartment had two bedrooms—one for him and one for Celeste to share with her sisters when they visited. There were no social services or adoption laws in those days, especially in the chaos of war.

Life was still plenty hard, and Jim was out of a job a number of years and the girls shed many tears over their loss and adjustment to England. But Luther was always able to make them laugh. Always.

Every Christmas after that, we would meet at my house to exchange gifts and reflect on all we'd survived. Occasionally, Ethyl Brand would be in the country and stop by to see us. And always, at the end of the evening, I would sit with Luther and eat sweets until his snores echoed through the house, and then I would guide him to bed.

"Love you sweet, Luther," I would tell him. "Love you sweet."

"Love Mum," he would whisper back . "Love Mum."

ACKNOWLEDGEMENTS

To my family—Steve, Anne, Adam, Julia, and Erin—for congregating around Mom and Dad's bed in 2005 to marvel at a paragraph I had scribbled about a green alien. I'd misspelled almost every word. "Maybe he'll grow up to be an author," one of you suggested.

Thanks to the National WWI Museum and Memorial in Kansas City, Missouri for access to their unparalleled research library.

Thanks to my godmother, Robin Kaye, for lending me her knowledge of the publishing world.

Thanks to publisher Jennifer Geist for the opportunity to learn what makes a book marketable and to Grace Carlson for her graphic design input.

Thanks to publishers Brenda Bradshaw, Ph.D. and Ryan Crawford for initially voicing their enthusiasm for my manuscript.

Thanks to publishers Kristina Makansi and Lisa Miller for their experience and professionalism throughout the editing and design process.

ABOUT THE AUTHOR

Ryan Byrnes is a St. Louis native. His first foray into writing was founding the publishing imprint, Avency Press, where he wrote one illustrated chapter book, *The Adventures of Wheatail*, and four young adult fantasy novels in the *Son of Time* series. Since then, he has worked with a publishing company, a literary agency, and various aspiring writers seeking to self-publish. Ryan now lives in Iowa and is a college student studying mechanical engineering and English. Between work hours, he builds Mars Rovers with his roommates, plays with cats, and watches Wes Anderson movies.